CW01641972

THE CLOCK TOWER MURDERS

CARLOS JACOBI PI

BOOK 4

DAWN BROOKES

Dawn Brookes Publishing

THE CLOCK TOWER MURDERS

This novel is entirely a work of fiction. The names, characters and incidents portrayed are the work of the author's imagination, except for those in the public domain. Any resemblance to actual persons, living or dead, is entirely coincidental. Although real-life places are depicted in settings, all situations and people related to those places are fictional.

Paperback Edition 2025
Kindle Edition 2025
Paperback ISBN: 978-1-916842-56-4
Hardback ISBN: 978-1-916842-57-1

Cover Images: Shutterstock
Cover Design: John & Janet

PROLOGUE

"YOU'RE FREE TO GO NOW, OFFICER." AFTER removing more long locks from her forehead than PC Sara Ransom would have liked, the nurse finished sewing the head wound with eighteen stitches.

Sara swung her legs over the edge of the examination couch and took a few tentative steps, trying to maintain her balance while the light-headedness wore off. "Thanks, Ian."

Ian's dark green eyes sparkled as he flashed her a smile. "Looks like it's going to be another one of those nights."

Sara's fingers gingerly touched her forehead. "You're not kidding. I hope you don't have too many more of our guys coming through here, though."

Ian shrugged in a 'what will be, will be' kind of way, clearing away his trolley and preparing for the next patient.

Sara walked shakily to the door, hoping to conceal her distress from the kind nurse. He had more problems waiting for him in the waiting room.

"Remember to get some rest," he called after her,

removing the paper sheet from the couch and pulling down a new one for the next patient.

Upon entering the busy waiting area of the Leicester Royal Infirmary, she was pleased to see Gary, though not quite as pleased to see the on-duty supervisory officer.

"Good to see you're still in one piece," said Gary with a grin. "This is Sergeant Quinn, our lift to the station."

Sara had known there would be forms to complete. "Watch your lip, Hodge," Sergeant Quinn said. He must have known Gary, but Sara hadn't met the sergeant before. "Sorry about your injury, PC Ransom, but as Gary says, I'll take you both back to the station and we'll complete the necessary paperwork."

"Thanks, I feel better," she replied. Although she didn't feel better, she saw no point in overstating the matter. Perhaps her mother was right; her constant complaints about the state of Leicester meant she worried more than she should about Sara's safety. What if she no longer felt safe as a Black police officer? With civil unrest escalating, exacerbated by politicians cutting the number of officers on the beat, she might have to leave the force. The powers that be informed the force that many of the so-called demonstrations were being fuelled, or at least inflamed, by individuals determined to incite chaos through violence. Even demonstrators not intent on violence were becoming more aggressive, as tonight had shown.

"How are you?" she asked Gary as they followed the sergeant out of the Accident & Emergency (A&E) Department, ignoring rude comments from drunks in the waiting room. Sara was relieved to escape the noise. More drunks and a few handcuffed but injured rioters, accompanied by colleagues, were being brought in. A tall Black man shot her a foul look. She sighed. Why do people have to be like this? Why can't they just get along with each other?

Gary replied, "Not bad. It just took a smidgen of glue to fix mine." He grimaced as he glanced at her bandaged head. "They really got you, didn't they? Do you think they meant it?"

She tensed, recalling the moment the attacker skirted around Gary to reach her. "Oh yes. They meant to teach me a lesson."

"Why?"

"You know why," she replied. "Don't start with the political correctness. To them, I'm neither black nor white."

Gary frowned. "Are you sure you're not reading too much into it?"

"To some in my community, I'm a traitor, and to your lot, I'm a legitimate target." Sara sometimes found herself echoing her mother's opinions rather than expressing her own reality.

"Let's not divide ourselves into separate groups, Sara. We're a team, and they're just mindless idiots, that's all," Gary said.

"On that point, we agree." Sara was too tired to argue.

"I'll give you a lift home once we're finished at the station," he said as they climbed into the back of Sergeant Quinn's patrol car.

"I'm not going home like this. My mum will have a fit. I'll ring her and tell her I'm working late, which is partly true. What time is it, by the way?"

"Uh," Gary checked his watch. "3 a.m." He gave her a sly look.

"Blimey. In that case, I won't call, I'll text. Hopefully, she's fast asleep in bed."

"She'll have heard about the trouble and will be worried. It's all over the news. You should phone."

Sara shook her head, which brought a new level of pain from her wound. "Mum avoids listening to it these days. She says she'll deal with whatever comes her way when it arrives. By that, she means you knocking on the door with bad news." Sara tried to laugh; her job caused her family real heartache. She changed the subject. "How are things out there now, Sergeant Quinn?"

"A fair amount of collateral damage: cars set on fire and general mayhem initially. The police support unit has calmed things down and moved people out of the centre. Last I heard, the surrounding streets were quieting down."

They went to the nearest station, where all the paperwork was completed. Once Sergeant Quinn was satisfied that he had filled out all the forms, he smiled. "I suggest that you two go home."

"Thanks," said Gary. "Come on, Sara, let me give you a lift."

When they were out of earshot of Sergeant Quinn, Sara shook her head. "No need; I'll hang out here for a while and grab a coffee. We never did get that break."

"Nope."

Sara and Gary Hodge had been about to leave the city centre when a rowdy gang of youths appeared, brandishing placards. With no official demonstration registered and no extra police presence, it was clear they were looking for trouble. Just as Gary called for backup, Sara caught sight of a glint from a broken bottle before it shattered against her head. She briefly locked eyes with her attacker and thought she recognised him, but he wore a mask, and the incident unfolded too quickly for her to be certain. Drawing her baton, she struck the assailant on the thigh while Gary pulled her out of harm's way. At that moment, someone assaulted Gary. Fortunately, reinforcements arrived just in time.

The two were rushed to A & E while their colleagues intervened, as they had needed to do all too often over the past couple of months: isolating the worst offenders and separating them from the rest until calm was restored.

Sara waited three hours for the nurse to stitch her up. According to the doctor who examined her before referring her to the nurse, the nights in Leicester were now similar to those in the 1970s when there had been a lot of violence. The doctor had been in his sixties, with battle-worn, weary grey eyes reminiscent of her father's before he left for the pub one night and never returned.

Sara and her mother had fought countless battles both before and since Sara joined the force, her mother supported by her two brothers. "You might as well put a target on your back. You're not one of them, and you won't be one of your own kind."

She constantly hoped they were wrong. However, recently, each day she donned her uniform, she prayed people would be better than that. They were not. On her less cynical days, Sara dreamed it wouldn't always be like this.

"Sara? Are you okay?"

"Sorry, Gary, I'm miles away. Go home to your fiancée; otherwise, she's going to believe the rumours that you and I are having an affair."

Gary smirked. "Wouldn't be such a bad thing. It might make her more interested."

She giggled. Gary was the best partner. Sara loved him like a brother, but they were not the slightest bit attracted to each other. "Be off with you. You know she's the only woman you've ever wanted."

"True. But I'd still like to be sure you're in a safe place tonight. Are you sure you don't want a lift?"

"Positive. I'll get changed, have a coffee, and then head to Suki's to bunk down there for the night. I've got a key, and as she's one of the few of my old school friends still speaking to me, I like to keep up with her."

"I've never understood this black- and -white thing," said Gary.

"That's because you're white," she replied. "And you've never been on the receiving end of racist police brutality."

"Oh, come on, Sara. Don't do that. You're starting to sound like them."

She smiled at him. Gary would never understand, and why should he? None of these issues should depend on a person's skin colour, their job, or any other nonsense like that. He epitomised everything that was non-racist. She hugged him. "Go home, Gary."

"All right, home it is then." They parted at the male and female changing rooms. "I'll see you tomorrow."

Sara sighed. "Let's hope it's quieter."

"See you, Sis." Gary's pet name for her brought her back

to reality, and she appreciated it. They made excellent partners.

After Gary left, Sara changed out of her uniform and removed the bandage from her head, as it was uncomfortable. Ian had covered the stitches with a dressing, which would suffice. She helped herself to a coffee, checked the local news, and learned that the streets in the town centre were clear, just as Sergeant Quinn had said. She needed air, so she decided to walk to Suki's house.

On her way into town, she stopped at an all-night café. As she entered, a few patrons cast sideways glances at her, but most ignored her. She felt safe here, as some of them were informers who didn't acknowledge her.

After consuming the unhealthiest meal she had eaten in a long time and wiping the grease from her hands and face, she stepped back onto the street. It was 5:30 a.m., and a chill filled the air. Walking through the city at this hour might not be safe, but having foolishly declined Gary's offer of a lift, she kept to the shadows.

Sara passed a few rough sleepers, tiptoeing so as not to disturb them.

Once again, her mum's anxious voice echoed in her mind. Stay out of my head, Mum.

As Sara approached the town centre, the damage left by the rioters became clear. She spared a thought for the people who would have to come in and clean it all up before the city awoke for another shopping day. The city cleaners were probably on their way right now.

The iconic clock tower loomed ahead, its shadow instilling a sense of familiarity. Almost there. Suki rented a flat above one of the shops, and Sara had a spare key. Her need for respite after a hard shift was becoming all too frequent. Sara knew that soon she would have to leave home, if only for her mother's sanity. But it would be a wrench for both of them. This night had been bad, perhaps the catalyst for her to seek alternative accommodation.

As Sara entered the square, the landmark clock tower, adorned with the faces of the city's benefactors, stood as it had for centuries – a reassuring presence that must have witnessed thousands of life's joys and catastrophes. She had met her first boyfriend near the tower, as countless couples had over the decades. Although she had been stood up a few times, she opted not to dwell on those memories.

Something caught her eye as she drew closer, causing her heart to race. She approached a person who appeared to have fallen asleep, intending to wake them on. Vagrants sleeping near the clock tower put themselves in danger. Some yob could easily kick their head in for fun. But as Sara got closer, she thought she recognised the woman. Could she be someone Sara had arrested in the past? If so, she couldn't recall her name. Sara gripped the woman's shoulder.

"Wake up. You can't stay here." The clean-up operation would happen soon.

The woman flopped backward, her eyes staring but unseeing. Sara reached for her phone to report the death.

1

CARLOS PARKED HIS CLASSIC FORD CAPRI IN THE car park behind his office and walked inside with his faithful Springer Spaniel, Lady. As he entered, he recognised familiar voices coming from the front.

At the sound of a well-known voice, Lady bounded ahead, her tail wagging enthusiastically as she let out delighted whines.

"Hello, Lady! It's so good to see you!" Fiona Cook exclaimed, her voice brimming with warmth.

Carlos stepped into the office, waiting for Lady's ecstatic whines to settle as she basked in the attention. His PA, Julie Stacey, had already put the kettle on.

"Fiona, it's great to see you," Carlos said, observing her closely for signs of bereavement. "I was so sorry to hear about your father."

Fiona lifted her gaze from stroking Lady's ears. "It was peaceful in the end."

"How was the funeral?"

"It was... you know, a funeral. But he got a good send-off, and I scattered his ashes in Epping Forest, where he and Mum met."

Carlos sat in an armchair, surrounded by walls lined with filing cabinets and shelves filled with crime investigation and forensics books. Fiona was already settled in another of the comfy armchairs where they received clients. Carlos's desk faced the entrance to High Street, while Julie's desk was nestled next to the large front window.

Julie re-entered with a tray bearing two coffee mugs and a plate of biscuits. Lady, having decided her welcome had been sufficient, wandered over to her water bowl and lapped it dry. They had been for a run before arriving at the office, and Julie filled another bowl with the dog's breakfast.

"You really shouldn't spoil her like that," Carlos remarked.

"She has to eat," Julie replied with a grin. "I'll crack on with the paperwork you sent through." With that, she left them to chat.

With Lady calmed and settled close to Fiona's feet, as if sensing her grief, Carlos addressed the elephant in the room. "Did your brother see your father?"

"Yeah, he made it down in the end. Not that he was of much use."

"Don't tell me he's back on drugs," Carlos said.

"No, nothing like that. He's just hopeless in these situations. He doesn't handle stress well, as you're already aware. But he seems to have got his life together. At least he's holding down an honest job."

Fiona's brother, Steve, had been living in Edinburgh for

a few years now. After spending some time with a crooked lawyer's daughter, he eventually realised he was being used and left, finding a job in a factory.

"I'm pleased he's staying away from the drug scene."

"Me too," said Fiona. Her life's mission revolved around solving crimes and protecting her younger brother, but criminals in high places had exploited that very commitment. However, Carlos and Fiona had previously worked tirelessly to expose corruption, managing to ensure the shady lawyer and Carlos's old nemesis, Terry Masters, were arrested and imprisoned. Just the thought of Masters made Carlos scowl as he reached for his coffee. "It's great to have you back in Leicester. Shall we do dinner sometime?"

Fiona's expression turned serious as she met his gaze.

"This isn't a social visit, is it?" His heart sank at the implication.

"Dinner would be nice, Carlos. But you're right. I need your help."

"Of course. What do you need?"

"Have you read about the unusual deaths of two sex workers?"

"The ones found leaning against the clock tower a week apart?"

Fiona nodded.

"Yes, but I thought you'd caught the perpetrator."

"We did. But it turns out we apprehended the wrong man. To be honest, Carlos, things haven't been great while I've been away."

"I've been following the headlines about the riots. In

fact, I almost drove into one that erupted out of nowhere but managed to avoid it."

"The truth is, the Force has been overwhelmed. While these women's deaths should have been a priority, there was a lot of other serious crime to deal with."

Carlos interpreted this to mean that the deaths of sex workers were considered a lower priority than other, more high-profile cases and had been pushed to the bottom of someone's pile. "But now that you're back, you've discovered they arrested the wrong person."

"Shortcuts were taken, but it was a simple mistake. The guy practically confessed, but it turns out he was one of those – how do I put it – fantasists. His neighbour informed us he has mental health issues and is a compulsive liar. Now we have another problem on our hands, which is where you come in."

Carlos set his mug on the table. "Go on," he urged.

"Word on the street is that there's a Romanian calling the shots in the sex trade."

"Nicolae!" The tension hit him like a bullet to the shoulder, and anger surged in his chest.

"I can't be certain, but from the descriptions we've received, it sounds like him."

Nicolae had been involved in murder and corruption and had been stopped while trying to leave the country during a previous shared investigation, but he had mysteriously escaped before being charged with any crime.

"How could he come back? Surely, he should have been arrested on entering the country."

"We don't have enough on him, Carlos. I told you that after he escaped, any evidence against him went missing."

"Very convenient," Carlos replied, initially pleased to see Fiona, but now the mention of the elusive Nicolae soured his mood.

"It's just rumours. No one has actually confirmed it's him. We've only heard chatter of someone in the background bringing more sex workers into the city."

"That sounds like part of his MO," Carlos said.

"I could use your help with these women's deaths. They thought they had someone, but since releasing him, the trail has gone cold. I'm having to start from scratch. Someone was covering for me while I was away, but let's just say he had too much on his plate and made mistakes."

"The thing is, Fiona," Carlos replied, "as much as I'd like to help, I'm joining Rachel in New York in a few days. You know she took a temporary job as chief of security on the Coral Queen."

"Yeah, I heard she finally saw sense and got away from you," Fiona laughed as she drained the remnants of her coffee.

"Ha ha," Carlos replied. "More like it was something she needed to get out of her system. They've been offering her that job for years. She needed a break from the force."

"I understand that feeling. Being a DI isn't all it's cracked up to be. There might be more money on the table, but it's three times the work."

"Not to mention the stress," he added. Noticing the lines beneath Fiona's eyes, he softened. "You're grieving, Fiona.

Can't you pass the senior investigating officer role to someone else?" Fiona had funded her father's care for years to ensure he received the best that money could provide, sacrificing her own needs in the process. But the guilt lingered, making her feel as though she had somehow let him and her brother down.

"They've covered enough for me, Carlos. If you can't do it, I'll accept that. You have no obligation to be involved." Fiona appeared conflicted for a moment, inhaling and exhaling deeply. She glanced over her shoulder to check if Julie was listening and, satisfied that she wasn't, took a deep breath followed by a slow exhale. "Nobody knows about this yet, and I'll be in trouble if anyone finds out you do, unless you agree to help."

Carlos waited for her to make her decision, trying to suppress his impatience. He sensed that whatever she was about to say would be pivotal, and she was grappling with her orders and her conscience about putting him under pressure.

"Another body was found yesterday morning."

Carlos's head snapped up. "It wasn't in the papers."

"We've kept a lid on it so far, but it will be headline news soon. A young PC discovered a woman's body at the clock tower. The officer had her head slashed with a broken bottle on Tuesday night. After being patched up, she was walking to a friend's house in the early hours when she came across the dead woman."

Conflict surged within Carlos. He wanted to see his wife, but he also felt an urgent need to put Nicolae behind bars and seek justice for three women who didn't deserve to die. Nicolae had become an unhealed scar; he was involved in everything from modern slavery and smuggling to the illegal dog trade, sex trade, and drugs. They had caught him a few years ago, but he had somehow escaped. Just when they thought they had rooted out corruption, all evidence against Nicolae mysteriously disappeared. He was always clever enough to use others to do his dirty work. Now he was back to his old tricks. "Okay. I'll do it, Fiona."

Lady's head shot up as if she understood the gravity of his promise.

Fiona stared at him. "Are you sure?"

"Rachel's on the Coral Queen for months. We'll meet in another place on her itinerary. I expect she's busy, anyway." He knew his wife would be disappointed if he chose not to go. As his own disappointment settled in, he almost changed his mind. There was nothing he loved more than being with Rachel. But Nicolae... His shoulders tensed again. Nobody would be more determined to put Nicolae away than he and Fiona, and she couldn't do it on her own; it was too dangerous.

"Thanks, Carlos," she said. "I really appreciate it. Please tell Rachel I'm sorry for upsetting her holiday plans."

"Are you sure you've got permission to involve me?" Carlos asked.

Fiona grinned. "I will by this afternoon. We need all the help we can get."

Carlos was well aware of the unrest in the city stemming from the Foxdale estate. It was an area he knew well, and he had recently uncovered the case of a missing daughter from an influential family. She had been groomed and forced into work as soon as she became addicted to heroin. Many young women found it impossible to free themselves, and increasingly, more were being trafficked from Europe. No doubt that was where Nicolae came in. Thankfully, the young woman he had found had agreed to enter rehab. Her parents would cover the costs, but he suspected it wouldn't be a long-term solution. Not until they cut off the head of the snake. Rachel had been a DI in the East Midlands but was attached to a different team from Fiona's.

The East Midlands Serious Crime Squad was large, but it was struggling to cope with the myriad challenges it faced. The region was vast and difficult to manage.

"Are you still on the boat?" Fiona had moved her houseboat to Leicester since she primarily investigated crimes in and around Leicester and Leicestershire. Rachel had dealt with several murders in Leicester, as well as in Derbyshire and Lincolnshire.

"Why wouldn't I be? She's had a makeover while I've been away. You'll have to come over one day."

Carlos recalled how cluttered Fiona's boat had been during his one visit. He wondered if, now that her care spending had ceased, she might consider settling for a house. It was far too soon to bring that up, he reminded himself.

"Let's start with a drink at the pub."

Fiona brushed biscuit crumbs from her jacket onto the floor, causing him to wince. "It's fine, Carlos. I'm sure Lady will clean up for you," she said with a laugh.

Carlos nodded at Lady, and she promptly did just that.

"I'll send you the files this afternoon. You can fill Julie in; I assume you'll want to use her for background checks."

"As long as you're happy to pay for her time and mine," Carlos replied.

"Please have her send over a contract, and I will ensure it's approved by the end of the day."

Carlos stood up and leaned down to hug Fiona. "I see you're still wearing the same raincoat."

"It's good to be working with you again, Carlos."

"Likewise."

"I'll send over the files for you to review as soon as I get back to the station."

For the next few hours, Carlos focused on finalising the paperwork for the case he had just completed to prepare for his trip to New York. After Julie left the office to pick up her daughter from school, he began reviewing the files that Fiona had sent him, dreading the conversation he needed to have with his wife. He calculated the time difference between the UK and Rachel's location in the Atlantic and picked up the phone with a heavy heart.

2

On Friday morning, the cold had woken Carlos at 6 a.m. He had spent the night in the apartment above his office, which was accessed by a secret door known only to a few people. The late October weather was unseasonably cold, a phenomenon Rachel had mentioned was occurring across the US as well. His wife had been understanding but disappointed when he cancelled their planned reunion. As he shook off his own disappointment, he got up and prepared to begin work on the case Fiona had asked him to assist with.

He messaged Fiona upon waking, asking her to arrange a meeting for him with PC Sara Ransom.

After a quick jog around Castle Gardens with Lady, a text came through:

'PC Ransom is on sick leave but happy to meet. Arranged for 10 a.m. at the Clock Tower, south side. Catch you later. Fiona.'

Carlos arrived ten minutes early and surveyed the clock tower from a distance. The landmark, which had stood since the nineteenth century, was a popular meeting spot in the city centre. It featured statues of four of Leicester's benefactors and had four clock faces, each facing a different compass point. His wife, being the historian in their relationship, had informed him that the building's architecture incorporated Gothic elements.

Having heard about Sara Ransom's injuries, he wasn't surprised that she had been given sick leave. Fiona had told him that her injury required eighteen stitches following an encounter with hooligans on Tuesday night. It had been an unusual night for a demonstration, but perhaps the intent was to strike when the police were least expecting it.

As he stood with Lady, scanning the area, he noticed a couple of CCTV cameras still covered in bright orange paint. His attention shifted when he spotted the woman he had been waiting for. She wore a hooded, thigh-length mauve jacket zipped to the neck, blue jeans, and Nike trainers. She approached the south side of the clock tower and checked her surroundings. Her hood partially obscured the dressing on her forehead.

"Come on, Lady. We're on," he said, giving the lead a brief tug. Lady became immediately alert. Sara's face was smooth, with high cheekbones and full lips, and he was pleased that the glass had not marred her attractive features. However, her eyes were sharp and disapproving, not returning his smile as he approached. The police were often wary of private investigators, much like they were of journalists.

"Miss Ransom?" He didn't wish to identify her as a police officer in public.

"It's Sara. I take it you're Carlos Jacobi?" her tone was curt.

Carlos tried a disarming smile. "Call me Carlos. This is my partner, Lady."

The corner of Sara's lips curled upwards as Lady introduced herself by nudging her head into Sara's right hand. Good girl, Lady, Carlos thought. Not everyone was fond of dogs, but he had trained her to understand when good manners were required.

Sara bent down and stroked Lady's head. "Partner, eh?"

"She's the only one willing to work with me," he said, extending his hand.

Sara shook it, appraising him with those sharp but searching dark brown eyes. "You're not what I was expecting."

"Not all PIs wear scruffy jackets and chew gum," he replied.

With Lady's help, Carlos sensed Sara was beginning to soften. "DI Cook asked me to meet you," she said. "How can I assist you?"

"Shall we find somewhere more private? My office is down the road, or I can buy you a coffee."

"Or there's a quiet bench just down there." Sara pointed to one of the many benches lining the High Street.

"Quiet bench it is, then. Come on, Lady." Carlos regretted not putting on his overcoat, as Julie had suggested when he left the office, but how was he to guess they would be sitting outside? "Before we go, could you just show me where the..."

He didn't need to finish his sentence. Sara had already anticipated it and was making her way to the north face of the tower. She stood a few feet away, pointing to a spot where a man was engaged in an animated conversation on his phone while drinking from a takeaway carton. Without asking the man to move, Carlos struggled to see clearly, not that it would have told him much, as the crime scene investigators would have already collected all relevant evidence and cleaned up. He had photos of the body as it had been found, along with a few of the crime scene.

"Seen enough?" Sara's question jolted him back from the images in his mind.

Just then, the man moved on. Carlos strolled to the spot and waited to see if Lady's ultra-sensitive nose detected anything while he looked around at all the street cameras. "Okay, how about that bench?"

Sara turned on her heel and marched away quickly. He guessed her age to be around twenty-three and then checked on his phone. Spot on. It might well have been the first body she had encountered. When they sat down, Sara was hugging herself, which could have been because of the east wind's chill or an attempt to shake off the memories of what she had encountered. Lady sensed it too and settled close to her new friend protectively.

"I'm not sure I can add anything to my statement," Sara said. "I assume you've read it."

Carlos nodded. "It's always better to hear it firsthand. If it's not too traumatic, would you mind walking me through everything that happened on Tuesday night, starting with the impromptu riot?"

Sara seemed surprised that he hadn't cut straight to the part where she found the body, but she answered the question. Initially, she started off in a monotone voice, describing how she and her partner had walked from the Jury Wall Museum along the High Street to the centre. "We were about to leave when a group of Black youths appeared out of nowhere."

"Now, if you think back, can you remember the direction they came from?" Carlos asked.

"From the old Market Street. It was odd."

"Odd how?" Carlos inquired.

"First, there was no demonstration on the radar, either unofficially or officially, and second, it was almost as if they had been waiting to ignite a flame."

"And you were the flame?"

Sara nodded, her eyes scrunched as she tried to recall what had happened on Tuesday night. None of this had been in her report, but Carlos wasn't sure whether that was because it had not been recorded or because she hadn't remembered at the time. "They were wearing balaclavas and black clothing. One of them came straight for me, bypassing my partner, Gary, and thrust a broken bottle in my face."

"He definitely bypassed your partner?"

"Yes. I figured it was because I'm a black cop. A lot of black people resent the police, especially—"

"Those of colour," Carlos finished for her.

"His eyes were full of hatred. I thought I recognised him,

but beneath the mask, it's hard to say. I'd know if I saw him again."

"What happened next?"

"I managed to reach for my baton and hit him across the legs. Gary radioed for help when they came running at us, and then he launched himself at the guy," Sara smiled. "Gary's not that big, but he's got the heart of a lion."

"Was he injured?"

"A minor cut, but help had arrived by then, and we were whisked to hospital."

"Do you think the guy targeted you because of your colour or because you're a woman?"

"It could have been either, since I'm bigger than Gary, but I reckon it was the former. Sometimes I think my mother's concerns about racism have made me biased, and I see things through her eyes. It's hard to be objective."

"I understand," said Carlos. "It's not the same, I realise, but growing up, we were the only Italians in our street and at our school. My sister struggled with it when we were younger. She lost all traces of her Italian accent. And then there's the name."

"It's Jewish, isn't it?"

"Yes, although I've never considered myself a Jew. My family wasn't religious, and now I'm more Christian. My wife's a Christian."

"The thing is, I encountered little racism growing up, but my mum bangs on about what it was like in the seventies, with racial violence every weekend. She's convinced it's all been simmering beneath the surface and that it's coming back. This latest unrest makes me wonder if she's right."

"I hope not," said Carlos. "And big cities all across the country have their share of weekend fighting. Do you have any idea what's sparked this latest round?"

"Why ask me?"

"Because you're a beat officer. And no-one knows a city better than those who patrol it."

"If you'd asked me last week, I'd have said it has nothing to do with racism."

"Why?"

"Because it feels more orchestrated. Although the riots seem to be triggered at random and cause significant damage, they feel contained."

"Like the spraying of the cameras and the rapid dispersal, you mean?"

"Exactly that," Sara said, slapping her head and wincing in pain. "I must stop doing that. But you're right. It's as if there's another purpose behind what appears to be random acts of violence."

Carlos was forming a picture in his mind and made a mental note to research what happened on the nights when the other women's bodies were found.

"You're doing great, Sara. Now, would you mind walking me through what happened after you left the hospital?"

"Gary offered to take me home, but I refused. My mum still doesn't know about this," she pointed to her head. "I have a friend who lives in a flat above the shop over there." Sara pointed to a flat overlooking the square where the clock tower was situated. "I was walking to her place because she lets me crash there whenever I need to."

"Are you still staying with your friend?"

Sara nodded again. "Until I can take the dressing off and comb my hair forward. Mum doesn't realise I'm on leave either, so don't go round there."

"I won't," said Carlos reassuringly.

"I saw someone sitting against the tower and assumed it was a rough sleeper. It was only when I tried to shake her, she fell back." Sara's eyes moistened.

"Take your time," Carlos said as Lady nestled closer to Sara.

"At first, I thought it was another sex worker I'd arrested because I recognised the face, but then I realised who it was."

"Councillor Whitwick."

"Yes, I saw her on the local television channel, saying she wanted to clean up this city once and for all."

Carlos was also aware of Councillor Jodie Whitwick, who in many ways was a religious crusader with strong convictions.

"My mum said she reminded her of Mary Whitehouse, whoever that was."

"She was a traditionalist, I believe," Carlos replied, "who took a stand against liberalism in the 1970s. My parents admired her stance, being devout Catholics."

"Well, I doubt Jodie Whitwick would be happy that my initial thoughts were that she was a sex worker." Sara smiled for the first time since Carlos had met her, a smile that lit up her face.

Carlos wanted to delve a little deeper into Sara's partner Gary, but the warmth and admiration with which she spoke about him warned him off. He would use other avenues for those inquiries. “Thank you for speaking to me. I realise this isn’t the norm, but Fiona – that’s DI Cook and I are friends and have worked together on some grim cases.”

“Sorry if I was a bit off,” she said, stroking Lady while holding his gaze. “I’d like to help if I can. I love this city and don’t want what’s going on to tarnish its reputation.”

Carlos handed her a card with his personal mobile number. “I’ll let you know if there’s anything else you can do. Call me if you remember anything else or hear anything on the grapevine.”

Sara took the card. “I will. Bye, Lady,” she said, stroking his dog’s ears.

3

Fiona was waiting for Carlos when he arrived back at his office.

"You look frozen," she laughed.

"Unlike you," he replied grudgingly, noticing Fiona seated comfortably in the warmth of his office with a mug of tea in front of her and her laptop open. "Sara was suspicious of me at first, so our meeting took place on a freezing cold bench."

Fiona laughed, then scrunched up her nose in sympathy. "That east wind's a killer."

"Don't remind me." Carlos moved over to the radiator for warmth. "What are you doing here, anyway? Thinking of moving in?"

"I told you to wear your coat," Julie scolded, but Carlos was grateful when she handed him a mug of hot tea before returning to her desk.

Fiona eyed him. "Don't get comfortable; we're going to the Foxdale Estate."

"Can't wait," said Carlos, taking a seat while Lady bounded around, greeting anyone who would give her attention. After receiving a quick stroke from Fiona, Lady lay down next to the radiator.

"Did you find out anything useful from your interview with Sara Ransom?"

Carlos reflected on the interview. "Maybe. We need to look back at the nights the other two women were murdered and determine whether these so-called riots are spontaneous or calculated to conceal what was to come later."

"It's interesting you say that because I've been wondering the same thing. I've got one of the DCs looking into it."

Julie looked up from her computer screen. "There were riots on both nights. I remember the reports in the papers mentioning sprayed CCTV cameras and suchlike, but there have been other nights of unrest."

"What else did the papers say?" Carlos asked. He always read and listened to the local news, as it often had a bearing on his work, but with serious crimes like these, he left it to the police and skimmed the articles.

"Not much. The first death hardly got more than a paragraph, while the second was more detailed, with a headline something like 'Second Sex Worker Butchered', or words to that effect."

"Neither woman was butchered," said Fiona, rolling her eyes. "Both died from drug overdoses, and until the second death, when our Mr Fantasist came into the picture, the Senior Investigating Officer (SIO) thought the woman had taken a dodgy batch of crack cocaine. It was the fact that they were discovered sitting against the clock tower that drew Serious Crime's attention."

"I've studied the pictures," said Carlos, opening a folder from his desk and placing the images in front of Fiona. "We've got one east, one west, and your latest, south-facing."

Fiona's eyes widened. "OMG! I've been too busy studying how poor the investigation has been so far. This could mean there's going to be another."

"That's what it looks like," Carlos said grimly, his mind still processing all the details Sara had shared with him about Tuesday night. "What do you know about PC Gary Hodge?"

A scowl crossed Fiona's face as she brushed back her wild hair with a flick of her wrist. "Other than he's a good copper who had to have his head glued on Tuesday night, not a lot. Please tell me you're not going down the conspiracy theory route again, Carlos, or we might fall out."

"You asked me to help with the case for a reason, Fiona. I'll ask uncomfortable questions whether or not we fall out. If I get it wrong, you can crow over me later."

"Fair enough, Carlos, but just don't go around upsetting people, all right?"

"You know me," he attempted to flash a charming smile, but it failed to work on Fiona any more than it had on Sara. Perhaps he should leave the charm offensive to Lady.

"This isn't a Terry Masters situation. There might well be someone orchestrating the unrest, but that doesn't mean it's a conspiracy. All I ask is that you bear that in mind."

"I will. I just want to understand why the attacker deliberately bypassed Gary Hodge and went straight for Sara."

"Surely that's obvious," said Fiona.

"Not to me," Carlos argued.

"She's a woman. Women are perceived as the weakest links; you know that as well as I do."

"Sara believes the attack on her was racially motivated," Carlos replied. However, he harboured a lingering doubt about why the man hadn't gone directly for Gary, who was closest.

"And she might have a point, though these riots haven't been race related. They've been more like something kicks them off for no reason. They are not confined to any one sector of the community."

"That's my point," said Carlos. "I don't think they targeted her because of her colour or her gender, but they may have wanted to make it look like either, or both."

Fiona scratched her chin with her thumb. "I see what you mean. You're not suggesting Gary's dirty, then?"

"Not yet," said Carlos, "but we can't rule that out. Sara received eighteen stitches, and he sustained a minor wound that required a small amount of glue to put right."

"Yes, while protecting his colleague, Carlos. I've read the report. He could have waited for backup, but he didn't. They make a good partnership. They've been together since she started. Their arrest rates are slightly above average, and there's been no hint of corruption. PC Hodge has been in the force for twelve years without a blemish on his record."

Carlos smiled. "So you have checked on him, then."

"Give me some credit, Carlos. I'm not an idiot. Of course, I've checked on both officers. From what I see, they just happened to be in the wrong place at the wrong time on

Tuesday night. Neither of them has been involved in any of the other riots. Gary Hodge is a good cop."

"Why no promotion?" Carlos asked.

"May I point out that not everybody wants the responsibility that comes with a more senior position? We have career beat cops who excel at what they do. I don't know Gary Hodge because I'm in serious crime and he's a beat cop. If it makes you feel better, I'll ask around, okay?"

"Remember to be subtle," said Carlos, teasing.

"Ha bloomin' ha," said Fiona, "you're the one who needs to be subtle. And I'd rather you focus on the investigation before you go down a blind alley trying to find more corrupt coppers. Now, are you ready or what?"

"When you've been stung once, you can't be too careful." Carlos drank the rest of his tea and placed both his and Fiona's used mugs in the kitchen.

When he returned, he looked at Julie. "Can you pull up the headlines from the nights when each body was found and then pull up every incident of unrest that has happened in the last six months? See if you can find a connection."

"I'll get right on it," said Julie.

"Can we go now?" Fiona gave Carlos a look that suggested he was living on the edge of her patience.

"Are you hungry or something?" he asked softly, remembering that she had recently lost her dad. Her sharpness might have more to do with the fact that she was bereft and had come straight back to what was, at best, a sloppy investigation. It was never fun having to start from scratch when a trail had gone cold. And now a vocal and prominent councillor in the city had been murdered. His suggestion that another murder could be imminent hadn't helped her mood.

Fiona grinned. "Actually, I am hungry. Let's grab lunch on the way." Carlos felt sure that would help. "We'll take my car," she added. "I'm not driving in that heap of junk you've got."

"It's a classic that I've painstakingly stripped and upgraded. I barely fit in your old Mini, you realise that."

"Then perhaps you'll try not to annoy me in the future. Just push the seat back and stop moaning." Carlos grabbed his overcoat from the coat hook in the back hall. Lady jumped up.

"Lady, you stay here with Julie," Carlos commanded.

Lady didn't look too upset about not joining him. She'd had a long run, and he didn't think she'd enjoyed sitting in the freezing cold High Street any more than he had. At least her coat was better suited to the weather.

"Don't worry, Lady," said Julie, giving Carlos a sympathetic grin as Fiona marched towards the back door. "I've got some treats for you in the kitchen."

"You spoil that dog," said Carlos.

"She's a good worker, and like all good workers, she deserves treats," said Julie. "Now be off with you before you're in trouble and let me press on with my work."

Carlos reluctantly followed Fiona through the back and into the private car park, where she waited impatiently. He hesitated for a moment before opening the passenger door. Fiona placed both arms on the roof, glaring at him. "Not a word, Jacobi. Not one word, just get in."

Although her tone was sharp, the sparkle in her eyes reassured him that the friendly Fiona was back.

4

Once Fiona finished a large and greasy lunch, while Carlos opted for the healthiest item on the menu, which was buttered white toast, Fiona drove them to the Foxdale Estate.

"You haven't told me who we're seeing," Carlos said as he tried to unlock his knees in the cramped space. Despite pushing the seat back as far as it would go, he was still too tall.

"A friend and coworker of the first victim. Angela Morris, as you will have gathered from the report, was a thirty-year-old mother of one, known by the street name 'Angel.' When a member of the public found her at the clock tower, she had a religious pamphlet pinned to her cardigan."

"I didn't read or hear anything about the religious pamphlet, but I saw it mentioned in the file."

"They kept that part out because the SIO assumed some 'God squad' type added the pamphlet after death."

"Why assume that, rather than considering it might have been a religious fanatic purging the streets?" Carlos asked.

Fiona shrugged. "It could even have been her last customer who killed her, for all they knew. Some people these women associate with are the biggest weirdos around."

Carlos believed it should have been mentioned in the news, in case anyone recognised the leaflet. Julie was trying to trace the organisation referenced. "What about the second victim? Did she have a similar leaflet pinned to her clothes?"

The annoyance on Fiona's face answered his question, but she nodded.

"Anyway, back to today. Most of the women who avoid pimps have a safety network in place. Angel belonged to a trio. The idea is that they check in with each other when they finish their shifts. Often, they let the others know where they're meeting clients." Fiona removed one hand from the wheel to make a single inverted comma with her index finger. "We're going to be speaking to a member of Angel's safety network. The other dropped out after Angel died and won't speak to us."

"You could make her."

"I could, but I don't want to go down that route yet. I'm sure we will, but first, let's talk to the one who is willing to speak to us. Her street name is Ruby; her real name is Rishka Galan."

"Is that Eastern European?"

"I'm not sure. It sounds like it, but many people of Eastern European descent are born in this country," said Fiona. "You can ask her when we arrive."

"Where are we meeting her?"

"Not at her flat, that's for sure," Fiona replied. "She wouldn't let us in without a warrant. I've arranged for us to meet her at Foxdale Baptist Church."

Carlos raised an eyebrow. "The minister there is a good guy, and he runs an outreach programme that welcomes people from any background. You'll like him."

"Does he have a name?"

"Paul Allen. There's a community annexe where clubs and outreach programmes are held, and it is also available to hire for parties and similar events. Paul has a dedicated team who assist women in distress or seeking to escape from pimps. The building, along with his congregation, has faced risks because of their efforts, but most local criminals respect him."

"Unless a new player like Nicolae comes into the equation," Carlos mused.

"You're right. Recently, the building's windows have been smashed, and some members of the congregation have received threatening letters. None as menacing as those directed at Paul Allen himself."

"Let's hope he doesn't provoke Nicolae too much," Carlos remarked.

"Even Nicolae is reluctant to involve the law. I believe they let a few sex workers slip away while playing the long game, as many return to their former lives."

"I look forward to meeting this Paul Allen."

"You'll get your chance, as Ruby has only agreed to meet us on the condition that he's present. I could bring her in and apply the full weight of the law, but I prefer to speak with her in a non-threatening environment. These women face threats daily from their punters or from pimps, so we are the least of their concerns."

"I agree," said Carlos. "It's best not to be confrontational. We need to earn their trust, which is clearly what the minister has accomplished."

"Thank you for that vote of confidence," Fiona replied with a smile as she turned into a car park.

Foxdale Baptist Church was a significant and sizeable conversion of a former warehouse. The old signage had been replaced with a white strip of laminate bearing the church's name in gold lettering. The exterior walls were brightly painted with various biblical scenes, save for one area where local youths had spray-painted crude messages.

"What was this place?" Carlos asked Fiona.

Before she could respond, a muscular man in his forties approached them.

"Fiona, it's good to see you again. I'm sorry for your loss. Please accept my sincere condolences. How are you?"

Carlos watched, amused, as the bear of a man with a shaggy red beard pulled Fiona into a hug.

"I'm doing okay," she replied when he finally released her.

"And you must be Carlos. Welcome, I'm Paul." Paul held out a large, hairy hand, which Carlos shook. He believed one could tell a lot about a person through their handshake. Some let go immediately as if they had been burned, while the nervous were clammy; however, Paul Allen's handshake was firm, confident, and warm.

"Pleased to meet you," Carlos said.

"Follow me," said Paul, leading them into the vast building. Inside, there was an open hallway with stairs to the right and two doors leading into a large hall where Carlos assumed the services were held. The usual notice boards and signs over fire escapes were present, but Paul bypassed the main rooms and guided them through a narrow hallway leading to the annexe. He stopped outside a door. "She's nervous, Fiona."

"Thanks for the warning. We'll go easy."

As soon as Paul opened the door, Carlos saw Ruby freeze like a deer in headlights. She was of medium height, busty, and certainly not dressed for the weather, but that wasn't unusual considering her occupation, he thought. He despised men that used women like Ruby to fulfil their fantasies, but more than that, he loathed the people who drew them into such a world.

Fiona signalled for Carlos to remain still while Paul crossed the room, whispering. "Ruby, these are the people we spoke about. You're not in any trouble. They just want to ask some questions about Angela."

Ruby stopped pacing and biting her fingernails and nodded. "I don't have long."

"I understand," said Paul. "Come in; let's sit down." He gestured for Carlos and Fiona to enter.

Moments later, they were seated around a rectangular table. Paul sat next to Ruby, with Carlos beside him, and Fiona opposite. "Rishka prefers to be called Ruby and doesn't welcome physical contact. I'm sure you understand." He glanced at Carlos, who nodded in acknowledgment.

"Ruby, I'm Detective Inspector Fiona Cook, and this is Carlos Jacobi. He's a private investigator assisting in the investigation of your friend's death."

"It's okay to call Angel Angela," Paul added.

"My colleagues arrested a man who confessed to killing Angela, but we've realised he didn't do it, so I'm afraid we've lost some time," Fiona explained.

Ruby did not look up from her fingernails, prompting Paul to urge Fiona to continue.

"I'm in charge of the investigation, and I wonder if you can tell me anything at all about the night Angela died?"

Silence.

"Take your time," Paul said as the silence stretched. The only sound in the room was Ruby's ragged breathing. In contrast, Paul remained as calm as a millpond. Carlos was impressed by the soothing effect the man had on both women. Normally, Fiona would be pulling her hair out by now, but she sat in silence, taking her cues from the minister.

"We were happy," Ruby finally broke the silence. "It had been a good night, and we earned more than usual for a Sunday..."

Carlos noted a flicker of a frown cross Paul's face and could only assume it was because of the mention of that type of work taking place on the Sabbath.

"I last spoke to Angel at 3:15 a.m. on the Monday morning when my client left. We checked in with each other at the end of our shifts. There was trouble in the city centre that night, and I told Angel to avoid it. She said she wasn't going out again, and that Princess was already safe. Princess is our other friend."

"Did Angel contact you to let you know she had changed her mind?" Carlos asked, keeping his voice low.

"No, but I switched my phone off. Some punters think

we should always be available, but I didn't need any extra money, so I went home to sleep."

"Can you think of any reason Angel might have taken a detour and ended up in the city centre?" Fiona probed.

Ruby shook her head, blinking away tears or fear; Carlos couldn't quite tell which. "Only if she received a big offer, but even then, she would have contacted one of us, and she didn't. Sometimes, though, she could be reckless."

"In what way?" Carlos asked.

"You tell them," Ruby said to Paul.

"The women have been warned to stay away from high-value clients in certain areas of the city, but Angel didn't always follow those rules."

"Who warned you away from these areas?" Fiona inquired.

Ruby shook her head vehemently. "These people are dangerous."

Carlos leaned forward. "Is that what you believe happened that night? That Angel went into one of these areas you were warned to avoid?"

"From where she was, she would have had to drive through that area to bypass the town centre, but she shouldn't have stopped. We warned Angel, and now she's dead." Ruby's hands trembled, and Carlos could sense her agitation.

"Do you have any names that might help us find her killer?" Fiona asked.

"Threats come third or sometimes fourth-hand, but if we went alone, we knew the rules. I can't tell you anything else." She shifted back in her chair, looking ready to run.

"Just one more question," said Fiona. "Was Diamond also a friend?"

"We met a couple of times. She didn't want to work with anyone, bragged that she had grown up with violence, and feared nothing. I wished I were like her until she ended up dead."

Carlos wanted to ask more questions, but Paul shook his head. "Thank you, Ruby. You know where to find me if you need help."

Ruby couldn't leave the room fast enough. It was as though she were being chased by a pack of hounds.

"Why did you stop the interview?" Carlos asked, annoyed.

"I have to maintain her trust, and she asked me to end it if I sensed she'd had enough. She's ready to leave this life behind, and I don't want to push her away when I can draw her in."

Carlos hoped the gentle giant sitting opposite him was right. He might not agree with his methods, but he couldn't deny his conviction.

"We appreciate you pulling this together, Paul," said Fiona. "Excuse my friend; he should have more understanding, considering his father-in-law is a vicar."

"Is that so?" Paul replied, beaming.

"He's a good man," Carlos replied.

"Anyway, Ruby couldn't identify who was responsible for the threats, but one person you need to speak to is Travis Fish. He's a former drug dealer and sometimes provides me with useful information when girls are in trouble."

"A dealer with a conscience," Fiona remarked. "Now, that's a rare thing."

"Former dealer, Fiona," Paul corrected.

"Where can we find him?" Carlos asked.

"If you're available, you can talk to him tomorrow. He attends an AA group every Saturday evening."

"Here?"

"In the annexe, yes. We don't run it, but we allow the counsellor to use the building for free."

"I take it the counsellor doesn't realise what Mr Fish did for a living," said Fiona.

"It's called Alcoholics Anonymous for a reason," Paul replied, "so I guess not. But at least he's not drinking."

"Is he still dealing?" Carlos snapped.

"Not as far as I understand. I've said all I can. I hope you find out who's responsible for this because I'm concerned about these women."

"And I worry about you," Fiona said, shooting Paul a tender look.

For a moment, Carlos wondered if these two had feelings for each other, but Fiona was already on her way out before anyone could say anything else. "Come on, Carlos. I've got to give a briefing in half an hour. Speak soon, Paul."

5

"How did you two meet?" Carlos asked as soon as they were back on the road.

"I arrested a member of his congregation for patricide."

"Please tell me you're joking."

"Paul doesn't judge people. If someone asks for help, he provides it. But when the guy confessed to what he'd done, he fulfilled his legal duty and reported it. Since the Senior Investigating Officer on the case was anti-religious, Superintendent Henley asked me to make the arrest. Our paths have crossed a few times since."

"Is he married?"

"Drop it, Carlos."

Carlos wanted to ask how their paths had crossed, given that she worked in serious crime while the minister ran a church, but he let it go. Fiona could do with a bit of luck, and a big cuddly bear wouldn't do any harm. Paul Allen seemed genuine enough, and if Ruby and Fiona trusted him, he would give him the benefit of the doubt.

Twenty minutes later, Carlos was hanging around on the edge of Fiona's briefing. She introduced him to the team working on the case. He had met a few of them before, like DS Hugh Barber and DC Barry King, who had been a PC until Fiona uncovered a corrupt officer and brought him in as a replacement. Fiona explained Carlos's presence by noting that the force was short-staffed and that he was an efficient pair of hands with whom she had worked before. There would always be those who resented a PI's involvement because of professional pride or for other reasons. More than anything, Carlos hoped there were no remnants of the turbulent days under Terry Masters' corrupt influence. There might still be a few working for the wrong side, and Nicolae had a habit of buying officials from across the spectrum of public services.

While Fiona updated the team on what they had discovered thus far, Carlos's mind wandered back to the missing evidence against Nicolae. He surveyed the room. Someone had deliberately made that evidence disappear. Was that person in this room? Or worse, were they keeping Nicolae informed about the investigation's progress – or lack thereof? Had the initial investigation been a case of incompetence or conspiracy? After the arrest of a former DCI and others in his close-knit team, Carlos maintained a healthy – or as Fiona would say – unhealthy suspicion of corruption when it came to incompetence.

"I want extra patrols around the Foxdale Estate until this killer is found," Fiona said.

"Are you suggesting the councillor's death was a case of

mistaken identity, Ma'am?" one of the newer DCs, whom Carlos hadn't met before, asked.

"Councillor Whitwick had been working late on Tuesday night; perhaps she witnessed something that led to her death. Therefore, I'm not ruling anything out, but I want women working out of Foxdale to be protected," Fiona replied.

A slight murmur arose from a trio sitting near the DC who had asked the question, each receiving a stony glare from Fiona. They had misjudged the SIO if they thought she would tolerate prejudice. "You, DC Maplin." She pointed at the questioning DC. "Take a patrol car and work with PC Gary Hodge. I want you to conduct door-to-door inquiries in the neighbourhoods where sex workers meet clients. Show the deceased women's photos and ask if anyone saw anything on the nights they were killed."

"But Ma'am—"

"Starting now," Fiona interrupted.

As the disgruntled DC left the room, Fiona turned her glare on the other two. "Anything useful to add?"

"No, Ma'am."

"Good. You two can go through all the statements and evidence from the first two deaths and have everything ready for me before you go home tonight or by Monday morning. I want anything we missed." Neither argued. Carlos recognised one of them from a previous investigation but couldn't recall his name.

"Tomorrow, Jacobi and I will speak to Travis Fish, a former dealer who might have known the women. If any of you find anything, contact me. And be warned, the local newspaper is running a big spread on Councillor Whitwick and the first two women's deaths tonight. I don't know how we held them off for this long, to be honest, but it seems they owed us one." She glanced at Carlos.

Tony Hadden was a journalist he had shared intel with in the past. Hadden had been severely injured in a car crash while assisting Carlos, and they had since done favours for each other. Now a widely respected freelance journalist who wrote regular high-profile articles for the local newspaper and had contributed to several national newspapers over the past couple of years, Tony continued to share information to their mutual benefit. Fiona couldn't broker deals like that, but Carlos could, and when it resulted in mutual gain, such as exclusives like this one, Tony always kept his word.

"What happened to Angela's child?" Carlos asked when they got back inside Fiona's car.

"She'd been living with Angela's mother for the past few years, so it looks like the grandparents will raise her. The relationship between mother and daughter wasn't good, but they love their granddaughter."

"At least that's one good thing to come out of this sorry mess," Carlos said, shifting in his seat to find a comfortable position for his legs. "Where to now?"

"We're going to see Diane, aka Diamond Foster's ex-husband, and then I have meetings with the superintendent and my DCI. I'm not sure how much we'll get out of him, but it's worth a try. Diamond didn't seem to have any friends."

"When was she married?"

"Married at eighteen, divorced at twenty. I'm hoping he

can tell us how she ended up doing what she did, and if she had any friends we haven't heard about," Fiona explained.

"Good plan," Carlos replied, though he doubted that an ex-husband from years ago could help. "What was happening with your team back in the incident room? I noticed a few dissenters."

"Don't read too much into it. There are always some in every team. A few men just don't enjoy having a woman boss, and others, like Caroline Maplin, don't like any boss at all. She'd like to fast-track her way to the top."

Carlos chuckled. "You'll whip them into shape in no time."

"Let's just say it was a work in progress before I went on leave, and now they've become sloppy again. They're not a bad lot if kept busy; they just need direction. Once assigned tasks, they work hard. You know the expression about idle hands."

"A very true one," Carlos agreed.

"So, they only get up to mischief when they're not working."

"I doubt you'll give them much opportunity for mischief then," Carlos said with a sideways grin.

"You're right there, Carlos."

They hit a busy stretch of road, requiring Fiona's concentration, so they travelled in companionable silence for a while. Carlos was putting together the information they'd received about Angela's death and what Ruby had said regarding her disregard for rules.

"What do you think is going on here, Carlos? Lay it all out there."

"It's hard to say. You could have some nutcase with a grudge against sex workers. It wouldn't be the first time, although they are more protected these days. It still happens, especially since Angela – and it seems Diamond even more so – were working independently. Have you interviewed the father of Angela's baby?"

"She got pregnant at sixteen, and the father's long gone. He's not a person of interest. What do you think about Jodie Whitwick's death?"

"She could have been mistaken for a sex worker."

"I doubt that. She was wearing a two-piece business suit."

"Don't some of the high-class workers dress that way up here? They do in London, with posh flats and sports cars."

"Fair enough," Fiona conceded. "I can't see it, but that's one theory. What else have you got?"

"The first two deaths could have been staged to make it look like there's someone out there with a vendetta against sex workers, while Mrs Whitwick was the target all along. I assume you've checked her husband?"

"I've been wondering about that side of things, and yes, her husband has an impeccable record and was in Amsterdam until we called him on Wednesday to inform him of his wife's death," Fiona replied.

"Not in the red-light district, I assume?"

"Not funny. What we understand is that Jodie Whitwick and her husband, Andrew, have strong religious convictions. Jodie was unpopular with the liberal elements of the community; some saw her views as extreme, even bigoted. So take your pick of the groups she alienated."

"Did she rub anyone else up the wrong way?" Carlos was trying to connect the dots to determine if Nicolae could have been involved in these deaths or if he was not part of the picture at all.

"I haven't got on top of that yet; I'll be working through the paperwork over the weekend. Maybe you could ask Julie to help?"

"Good idea, but she'll be finishing soon," said Carlos as he called his personal assistant.

"Hello, Carlos. How did the interview go?"

"It was useful, although all we found out was that Angela might have strayed into an area that independents weren't supposed to enter. Fiona's got her team rechecking the CCTV footage from where she was when Ruby last spoke to her to see if they can trace her movements. As you know, her car was found burnt out a few days after her death. We're on our way to speak to the second victim's ex-husband. There's a lot more to do. How was your morning?"

"You're right about the riots occurring on the nights of the murders, but we already knew that. The interesting thing is that none of these riots erupted from organised demonstrations."

That aligned with what Sara Ransom had told Carlos earlier.

"Nobody saw it coming. All the other spikes of unrest had a clear trigger."

"I'm putting you on speaker, Julie. Fiona's driving," Carlos said as he pressed the button.

"There were two other occasions when it seemed trouble

sparked out of nowhere. Your reporter friend provided me with that information."

"Tony?"

"Yeah, he gave me a heads-up when I mentioned what I was looking into. As you asked me to provide him with some background for his article, we exchanged information. He mentioned that on the other two similar occasions, major crimes were committed."

"Such as?" Fiona asked.

"There was a jewellery shop robbery in the city centre, and the CCTV cameras were spray-painted or destroyed, just like on the nights the bodies were found next to the clock tower."

"I read about that. They thought it was an opportunistic robbery because of the riots." Carlos looked at Fiona. "You were on leave."

"Tony's suspicious of that conclusion. He suggested it was the other way around and that the riots were a distraction, allowing the thieves to rob the jewellery store while law enforcement was occupied with containing the rioters."

"Okay, it seems we're developing a theme here," said Carlos. "And what about the other one?"

"Not as serious, but someone broke into the council headquarters and stole documents. The offices were ransacked."

"What documents?" Fiona asked, beginning to look angry.

"Mostly information about the deceased councillor. Her home office was robbed on the same evening, but she dismissed it as merely idiots trying to intimidate her and advised the police to focus on more pressing matters, such as ensuring the city's safety."

"Sounds like her," said Fiona.

"Thanks, Julie. Things are starting to fall into place. While we're discussing Jodie Whitwick, could you do a deep dive into her background? She upset certain communities with her anti-prostitution and anti-immigrant stance, but did she antagonise anyone else? Is there something we're overlooking?"

"I'll start on that now. Are you coming back to the office?"

"Yes, but you'll be gone by then. Unless there's something that requires my immediate attention, please leave me a file in the hideaway."

"Okay. If I don't see you later, I'll see you on Monday. Do you want me to drop Lady off at your house, or are you staying in the flat tonight?"

"Leave her there. I'll take her out and feed her later. I might go home afterwards. I need a decent night's sleep and want to collect some fresh clothes to take to the flat. Fiona and I are interviewing a former drug dealer tomorrow night, and I might stay in the flat after that. Have a good weekend, Julie, and give my love to Freya."

"I will, and I'll do as much as I can before I leave."

Carlos ended the call.

"You have a great PA," said Fiona.

"She's excellent. Hiring her when I took over the lease was the best decision I made." Carlos had been fortunate to inherit Julie along with the office after the previous PI was murdered. He had moved from London to Leicester after tracking down the killer. Julie was thirty, trustworthy, and reliable. Her self-confidence had returned after she survived a failed relationship in which her ex left her with a three-year-old child. Freya was now seven and at school. Carlos offered Julie a flexible job that allowed her to balance childcare with work, something she had never attempted to take advantage of.

"Have you retired your London office now?"

"My business partner took it on, and he's doing well. It was too much for me trying to split myself in two running London and Leicester offices. Plus, I wanted to be closer to––"

"Your wife." Fiona's laugh filled the small space of the car. "The one who left you for a cruise ship."

"Hilarious. I've told you before, it's something she has to get out of her system. And may I remind you that if it weren't for you, I'd be flying out there this weekend?"

"Sorry." Fiona smirked.

"Yes, you look it. To be fair, Rachel and I didn't see much of each other before she left. We've always been ships passing in the night. But we love each other, and it works for us."

"You're a hopeless romantic, Jacobi. But you and Rachel make a good couple. My favourite type of relationship involves not seeing much of the other person."

"If we're discussing relationships, you haven't told me whether Paul Allen is married?"

"I thought I told you to drop it," Fiona replied with a grin.

"Okay, so where does Diane Foster's ex work?"

"In a pork pie factory... and don't go on about how unhealthy they are, because Leicester is famous for them."

"My lips are sealed."

"Yeah, right. Don't knock the pork pie business, although I believe they bake other things as well. I'm reliably informed that Leicester was once famous for hosiery, as well as crisps, pork pies, and biscuits."

"No wonder you love it so much," Carlos said, grinning. "I tried a pork pie once, and it made me feel sick."

"I don't think pork pies are meant for healthy bodies like yours, Carlos. They're more suited to the likes of me, and I love them, especially at Christmas."

"Can we return to the subject of Diane's ex?"

"Oh, yes. His name's Stefan Foster. Interestingly, Diane kept his surname, but then she didn't use her real name much because she lived under her street name. This is where we'll find him." Fiona swung right and stopped at the barrier of a huge bakery.

6

Fiona and Carlos waited at the barrier for one of the security guards to leave his hut and come out to the car. A heavy-set man leaned down as Fiona opened the window.

She flashed her ID. "I've got business inside. Could you open the barrier, please?"

The man gave a thumbs-up to his colleague, and the barrier opened. "Reception's straight ahead," the guard informed her.

"Thanks."

They drove through the expansive car park, taking some time to find a space amid the throng of vehicles. Eventually, Fiona squeezed into a vacant spot.

"Big business," Carlos commented.

"It would appear so," said Fiona. "Clearly, there's no early Friday afternoon knocking off here."

Carlos had been thinking the same but imagined that autumn was a busy time for bakeries like this, as people turned to comfort food to cope with the colder days and nights ahead. He was relieved to be released from the confines of Fiona's car and to stretch his legs.

Fiona took a call from one of her detectives, which allowed him time to stamp away the pins and needles and aches in his knees while surveying the unfamiliar building in this part of Leicester.

Once Fiona climbed out of the Mini, they started walking towards the main entrance, but she was already eyeing her watch. "We might be cutting it fine here, Carlos. I thought we'd be here earlier. My meeting starts in an hour, and these people will knock off soon. Perhaps we should wait until Monday."

Carlos wasn't keen on wasting time, especially since Diamond's ex might not have any information for them anyway. "We'll make it snappy," he replied, quickening his pace to a march.

Fiona's loud sigh reached his ears, but he pressed on. They entered the building, arriving at a large reception area with most of the doors to the right. While Fiona shifted from foot to foot, constantly checking her watch, the woman behind the desk answered three calls, routing each one to another part of the building. Concerned that Fiona might turn around at any moment, Carlos leaned over the counter, drawing the woman's attention. She ignored the next call and looked up at him. "How can I help?"

Fiona seized the initiative, flashing her ID. "I'm DI Fiona Cook, and this is my colleague, Carlos Jacobi. We'd like a word with Stefan Foster."

The woman's eyes widened in alarm.

"Don't worry," Carlos said, "he's not in trouble. We just want to ask him a few questions about someone he used to know."

"Oh, okay. Let me just make a call. He's on the floor somewhere." The woman, whose name badge read Trisha, tapped a few keys before picking up the phone. "Can you tell Stefan a detective wants to ask him some questions? No, nothing like that... it's nothing he's done... Right, I'll send them through." She glanced at Fiona and Carlos. "Go through that door, and he'll meet you inside."

Fiona and Carlos took the first door on the right and pushed it open as Trisha buzzed them through. They were almost immediately met in the corridor by a man in his mid-twenties, wearing white overalls and a net hat covering sandy brown hair. Stefan was around five feet seven and overweight. His ruddy complexion flushed darker as he stared at them with wide green eyes and furrowed eyebrows.

"Don't worry, Mr Foster, you're not in trouble," Fiona reassured him, briefly introducing herself and Carlos before continuing. "We need to ask you a few questions about your ex-wife, Diane."

"I haven't seen Diane in six years, but I read she died. Was it an overdose?"

"We're keeping our options open at the moment," Fiona replied. "Did any of my colleagues interview you after her death?"

Stefan stroked his chin. "No. But I didn't expect them to. As I said, Diane and I weren't in contact."

"Is there a place we can talk privately?" Carlos asked, not

wanting to conduct an interview in the narrow corridor, where Stefan was blocking their way.

"Oh yes, sorry. We can go to the canteen upstairs. There'll be a mass exodus soon when the bell sounds, except for those doing overtime."

Stefan led them through a long corridor and upstairs to a large canteen that was empty. "It's closed for food, but we come up here for breaks. The smokers go outside," Stefan explained.

Once seated, Fiona got straight to the point. "Have you had any contact with Diane or any of her, erm, colleagues?"

"There was no point. We went in opposite directions, as I'm sure you realise. Fool that I am, I had no idea she was in that game until a year after the divorce."

"Were you surprised?" Carlos asked.

Stefan's gaze was fixed on the table before he answered. "Not when I heard she was driving an MG. Diane was always ambitious, and obviously her line of work brought in more money than I could provide."

"She wasn't a sex worker when you were together?" Fiona asked bluntly.

Stefan's face flushed an even darker crimson. "Of course not, but she wanted more than I could give her."

Carlos discreetly kicked Fiona to ensure she didn't make any inappropriate comments, but she remained silent.

Stefan continued, "She said I lacked drive. I've never been ambitious, even though I am a supervisor now," he said proudly. "Diane wanted the high life and resented the way we lived in a two-bedroom rental. With my paltry earnings, as she called them, she complained we would go nowhere.

When I look back, we were never suited; the only reason she married me was to escape from her stepdad. She hated him."

"Did she keep in touch with her mum or stepdad?" Carlos asked.

Stefan shook his head. "Her mum's an alcoholic, and her stepdad is in prison for aggravated robbery."

Carlos tried another angle. "Is there anyone from your old life that Diane would have kept in touch with?"

Stefan shook his head again. "Sorry. She looked down on everyone. Her only interest was in getting rich and look where that got her." He didn't sound bitter, more accepting. "You could always try the guy I suspect got her on the game."

Carlos sensed Fiona's exasperation as the table shifted slightly.

"Yes, why don't you tell us about him?" she said, dripping with sarcasm. Thankfully, Stefan, being a simple sort, completely missed it.

He scratched the back of his neck, looking uncomfortable. "His name's Travis Fish. He was always sniffing around Diane, telling her she could make something of herself. I never liked him, but she was flattered by the attention. He used to deal drugs around the estate, but I gather he recently got religion or something. Anyway, after Diane left me, I saw them together a few times. He had his arm around her, all protective-like. That was the last time I saw her, but we're going back years here, so it's a long shot."

"Do you know where we can find this Travis Fish?" Fiona asked, although they already knew where to find Fish.

"No idea. Like I said, I heard he cleaned up his act, got

sober and found religion." Stefan glanced at his watch. "Look, I need to get back to work. My supervisor's already going to wonder what's going on."

Fiona handed him her card. "If you remember anything else, please call me."

They watched Stefan disappear back through the door to the stairs.

"Well, that was illuminating," Fiona said, jumping up and making a quick exit down the stairs. They nodded to the receptionist as the bell sounded to signal the end of the shift. "Quick, let's move before we get caught in traffic."

They were soon packed tightly once more in Fiona's car, and she sped out of the space as throngs of people appeared from every direction.

Once on the road, Fiona continued, "It looks as though our friend Travis Fish was doing more than selling drugs."

"At least it ties in with what Paul Allen told us about him, and we know where he'll be tomorrow."

Fiona pressed down on the accelerator, driving like a crazed motorist. Carlos opted to let her concentrate on the road. He wanted to reach his office in one piece. Eventually, Fiona screeched to a halt at St Nicholas Circle. "We'll catch up later and meet tomorrow."

"What time's the AA meeting?"

"Seven-thirty."

"Speak later." Carlos had barely exited the car and closed the door before Fiona hit the accelerator and sped out of sight.

7

THE CAR PARK AT FOXDALE BAPTIST WAS FULLER than it had been the previous day. Carlos noticed several battered vehicles and a couple of newer ones that stood out, particularly a bright blue Mercedes. The evening had turned cold, and a fine drizzle misted the windscreen of his Capri. Fiona had opted to drive separately and go straight home after the interview; she had worked late into Friday despite there being no fresh developments. Her old Mini pulled up next to his car.

Carlos climbed out of the Capri, pleased he was wearing an overcoat, and pulled his collar up.

"That's Fish's," Fiona said, nodding towards a silver Ford Focus while locking her car. As always, she wore her pale blue raincoat. "He's had a few fines in the past," she continued without pausing for breath, "apparently, he drives like he's got something to prove. He was pulled over last month for doing fifty in a thirty zone."

Carlos smiled when she finally looked up at him. "Good evening to you too, Fiona."

"Don't be facetious. Looks like they're still inside. Shall we sit in your car?" she suggested.

"Good idea."

Carlos unlocked his car, and they climbed inside. Lady tried her hardest to squeeze between the two front seats to greet Fiona, who laughed at her attempt, patting her head. "Hello, Lady. Shouldn't you be strapped in?"

"She was, but I let her loose. I thought we were going straight inside, but I guess I wasn't thinking straight."

Fiona got comfortable as they watched the church, waiting for the meeting to end. Lady settled on the back seat, giving up trying to rest her head on Carlos's shoulder through the gap between the front seats. "I hope this isn't a dead end," said Fiona. "I hate cold trails, and my new DCI is on my back about finding the councillor's killer. He's under pressure from above."

Carlos bristled. "He's not bothered about the other women then?"

"Of course he is, Carlos. In fact, he and Superintendent Henley are fuming about the wasted time spent on the wrong guy."

"What's he like?"

"He's okay, but he's had to hit the ground running with far too big a caseload. He seems happy enough to give me a free hand on this case as long as I keep him informed."

DCI Malcolm Flatley had taken over after his predecessor was arrested on numerous charges of corruption, and so far, Carlos had heard nothing to suggest he was anything like Masters. Thank God.

At eight-fifteen, people began to filter out of the church's annexe, their collars turned up against the rain, and conversations mostly cheerful. A couple of loners gave Carlos the impression they might be struggling. They kept their heads down and hurried into the night.

Paul Allen stood at the door, shaking hands with each man and woman as they departed. Next to him, a middle-aged woman chatted with a few people before heading to the Mercedes. Carlos assumed she was the group facilitator.

"Blimey," Fiona remarked, "if I'd realised counselling paid so well, I might have been tempted to change professions."

Carlos observed another man in his late thirties leaving last. He had straggly hair and a lean, wiry frame, wearing a denim jacket over a hoodie. He moved slowly. Paul gave Fiona a subtle nod.

"That's him," Fiona confirmed.

They waited until Travis Fish was halfway to his car before stepping outside. "Stay, Lady." Lady let out a small whine and watched through the window.

"Travis Fish?" Fiona called.

The man froze before composing himself. He turned slowly, his face settling into a mask of wariness.

"Who's asking?"

"DI Cook. This is Carlos Jacobi, a private investigator. We'd like to have a word about your former line of work and about Diane Foster."

Travis's expression didn't change, but Carlos noticed his

jaw tighten. "I've left that life behind me, and I don't know anyone by that name."

"That's odd," Fiona said, moving closer. "Because her ex-husband told us you two were once close. He said you might be able to tell us how she got into the sex trade."

"He's got me confused with someone else. Can I go now?"

"We could do this down at the station if you prefer," Fiona said pleasantly. "But I thought you might want to keep it informal. Given your past, you wouldn't want to be seen as a snitch."

Travis glanced back at Paul, who was still hovering in the doorway.

"If Pastor Allen doesn't mind, here is fine," Travis said reluctantly. "What do you want me to tell you?"

"Shall we go inside?" Fiona suggested. The facilitator and the others had disappeared by the time they reached Paul. "Do you mind if we use the room?"

"Not at all," Paul replied with a smile for Travis. "I'll be in my office."

The annexe was warm, with seats arranged in a circle. Carlos guessed someone from the church would stack them with others at the side of the room. The table where they had sat with Ruby had been moved against a wall. Once seated, Carlos studied Travis, trying to work out whether he had genuinely turned his life around or if he had some ulterior motive for being involved with the church.

"Let's start with your knowledge of drug dealing on the Foxdale Estate," he said.

Travis laughed without humour. "As I said, I'm clean

now. I don't deal in that stuff anymore. I was never a user, but I drank too much before packing it in eighteen months ago. Whatever you're after, it has nothing to do with me."

"We're not here about drugs," Fiona said. "We're investigating three murders, and I think you realise that already. Two sex workers have been killed in recent weeks, and now a councillor. Each woman was murdered and then positioned at the clock tower."

A flicker of emotion crossed Travis's face. Fear? Guilt? It vanished before Carlos could be certain.

"I heard about it. Terrible thing. But I know nothing about murder."

"If you've truly changed, Travis, you'll be honest with us," Carlos replied. "You knew Diane Foster and introduced her to someone. Her ex-husband believes you may have been responsible for her decision to work in the sex trade."

"He's wrong. I have no idea what you're talking about."

Fiona moved closer, her voice firm. "Listen to me, Travis. You may have convinced yourself you're a new man, attending your meetings, but regardless of whether or not you're sober, three women are dead. You're connected to at least one of them. So you have a choice: either help us now, or I can make your life very difficult."

Travis stared at the ground, his shoulders slumping. When he spoke, his voice was barely above a whisper. "I'm trying to stay out of these things. I can't be involved in this."

"You're already involved," Carlos said, his tone softer than Fiona's. "But helping us might be the thing that keeps you *out* of trouble. It could be your chance to make amends for whatever happened. We've been told you cared about some of these women. Don't you want redemption?"

Travis rubbed his thin face with both hands, avoiding eye contact. "Give me a minute to think."

Fiona's gaze bore into Travis with unwavering intensity. Eventually, he met her eyes.

"Okay, I knew Diane," Travis began, his voice flat. "You already know I was dealing back then. She was ambitious and wanted more than Stefan could offer her. They were constantly arguing, and she wanted out of the marriage. I introduced her to someone, telling her he might help her."

"Who?" Fiona demanded.

"I only knew him as Mr Cross. He had money, drove a Bentley, and wore expensive suits. Someone gave me his card and said he was looking for girls with potential. Girls who wanted to better themselves. For every referral, he paid me a hundred quid."

Carlos's stomach tightened as he glared at him.

"I'm not proud of it," Travis sank deeper into his chair.

"What happened to these girls with potential?" Carlos snapped.

Travis avoided his eyes. "He wined and dined them, made them feel special. Gave them money for nice clothes and took them to fancy restaurants. Then he introduced them to his friends. Wealthy men who wanted... company."

"And then?" Fiona's voice was icy.

"Then he got them hooked. Cocaine mostly, and I supplied it. Once they were dependent, he owned them. They would do anything to keep the supply coming. He set a few up in flats, made sure they had regular clients and enough drugs to feed their habit without going too far. They lived well. High-end, you know? But they were trapped."

"You knew this, and you still introduced women to him?" Carlos couldn't hide the disgust in his voice.

Travis's head snapped up, his eyes flashing with anger and shame. "I was in a terrible place, all right? I told myself the girls were going to end up in the trade anyway, and they knew what they were getting into. It was their choice."

"But it wasn't, was it?" Fiona interjected. "Not once they were addicted to drugs."

"No." Travis's voice cracked. "It wasn't. When I saw the state of some of them, I got out. That's why I'm here, trying to make something out of the mess of my life."

Carlos exchanged a glance with Fiona. This was bigger than they had thought. Not just individual murders, but a systematic grooming and trafficking operation. Had the women left Mr Cross's control only to be murdered as a result?

"How many women did you introduce to Mr Cross?" Carlos asked.

Travis hesitated, then nodded. "Not many. He was fussy about their looks and lifestyle. The last person I introduced to him was Angel, Angela Morris. About three years ago."

Fiona inhaled sharply. "So that's two of the victims."

"I didn't realise they were dead until I read it in the paper," Travis said quickly. "I swear I had nothing to do with that. I've been—"

"Yeah, so you said," Fiona replied, clenching her fists in her lap. Carlos could see she was trying to maintain control. "What have you heard about them since word got out?"

"Nothing. Look, the only reason I'm able to stay free is by keeping my mouth shut. I've already told you too much."

"What about Jodie Whitwick?" Carlos asked. "The councillor. Did she know about Mr Cross?"

"The anti-prostitution woman?" Travis's brows furrowed. "Why would she?"

"She was the third victim," Fiona said. "Found in the same way as the other two."

Travis went pale. "All I know about her is that she campaigned hard against a lot of things that made her unpopular, including the sex trade. It's common knowledge she was making noises about ending prostitution rings and threatening to expose people involved. There were rumours she'd been collecting evidence, but I think she was just trying to get noticed, you understand?"

"Well, she certainly did that," Fiona snapped.

"If she meant it, I can tell you now that some people wouldn't like it."

The pieces clicked into place. It explained the ransacking of her offices and home. "So she might have been getting close to your Mr Cross?"

"Not to Cross, but perhaps to whoever's in charge now," Travis said. "Mr Cross ain't around anymore; he disappeared about eight months ago. Just vanished. The girls he had set up were left to fend for themselves or were picked up by pimps."

"Do you think Cross is dead?" Fiona asked, her brow furrowed.

Travis shrugged. "I don't know what happened to him. But someone different is running the operation including the grooming and the high-end stuff. I hear things, even though I'm out of it. Before Mr Cross disappeared, I understood that someone new – someone dangerous – had come to town. That's all I'm going to say."

"Nicolae?" Carlos asked.

Travis's eyes widened. "I don't recognise the name."

"We've been after a man named Nicolae for years," Fiona said grimly. "Tell us what you do know."

"Not much more than I've already told you. The guy's connected to everything Mr Cross ran drugs, girls, smuggling. The high-end prostitution ring is just one part of it, but this guy's clever; he keeps his distance and uses intermediaries. I was already out of the game when he took over, but even those still involved have never met him."

"Could Mr Cross have been working for this man all along?" Carlos asked.

"Maybe. I never made the connection, but it's possible. The operation was too smooth, maybe too professional to be just one person."

Fiona leaned her elbows on the table. "We need a name. A real name for this Mr Cross character. And we need a name for who's running things now."

"I don't have his real name," Travis said. "I swear. He paid in cash and used burner phones. One of his former girls might have an idea."

"Well, since two of them are dead, who?" Carlos could sense that Fiona was tiring of Travis Fish.

"Maybe Princess. She worked with Angel and Ruby but dropped out of the group after Angel died. She was one of Mr Cross's girls originally. If anyone knows who he really was, it would be her. She was his favourite. In fact, now that I think of it, the other two were his favourites as well. He kept them away from the really dangerous clients."

Fiona pulled out her phone and scrolled through her notes. "Princess. Real name Priscilla Miles. We spoke to Ruby yesterday, and she told us Princess wouldn't talk to the police."

"She won't," Travis agreed. "But she might talk to Paul. She trusts him. He got her away from a violent pimp a couple of years ago."

"Can you arrange a meeting?" Carlos asked.

Travis hesitated. "I don't have her contact details. You have to understand, these women value their privacy, and right now, they are terrified. This new guy's people have eyes everywhere. For all I know, one of his people could be planted in Pastor Allen's congregation. If they think someone is talking..."

"We'll protect her," Fiona said. "We'll protect anyone who helps us."

"You can't protect them," Travis said quietly. "That's what Diane thought. She told me she planned to escape; she bought drugs from the new dealers to make them believe she was still hooked, but she was off them. She wanted to make enough money to disappear. But you can't disappear from these people. They find you."

Carlos thought of the three women, strategically positioned around the clock tower like a grim message. "Was Angela also trying to get out?"

"I don't know, we weren't in touch. Diane rarely confided in anyone, but she mentioned something the last time I saw her. She said she had information that could bring down the entire operation, which she might sell to the papers."

Fiona looked at Carlos. "I hope she didn't try to blackmail Nicolae."

"I told her she was crazy, that she should go ahead with her original plan, or she'd get herself killed. Maybe she didn't listen, Diane was hungry for wealth. It's all she ever wanted. I didn't believe she had anything substantial because if she had, the newspapers would have paid her for the story."

"When did you last see Diane?"

Travis's shoulders slumped. "Two weeks before she died."

Carlos ran his hand through his hair. "And Angel?"

"I've already told you we weren't in touch. But Angel was different from Diane. I can't imagine her being interested in bringing anyone down. She liked the money that came with the job. But Diane kept in contact with her. If someone thought Diane had told Angel about the information she had..."

"Angel could have been seen as a threat," Fiona finished. "And now they're both dead."

"What about Councillor Whitwick?" Carlos asked. "How else does she fit in?"

Travis shook his head. "If she found out about the grooming operation, maybe someone wanted to shut her up. Or perhaps they thought Diane had sold information to her. She wasn't popular."

Fiona straightened. "We need to find out what, if any, evidence Diane had and what Jodie Whitwick had compiled.

And we need to talk to Princess before something happens to her."

"You'd best reach out to Princess through Paul," Travis said. "But it might not work. She'll be spooked, and from what you're saying, she should be scared."

"If you can contact her, as well as Paul, and tell her we'll look after her," Fiona said. "If our theory about the clock tower positions is correct, there's going to be another murder. And soon."

Travis stood up, his face grave. "I can't make up for what I did. Introducing those girls to that life and I don't have Princess's contact details. But if I can help, I will."

"Help us find the guy who's running things. We're pretty sure it's Nicolae," Carlos said. "Help us stop this before anyone else dies."

"I'll do what I can," Travis muttered, unconvincingly. Carlos knew men like Travis Fish would only look after themselves, it was unlikely he'd risk his newfound life to help them.

Fiona interrupted Carlos's thoughts. "What do you know about the riots?"

"Nothing as such, but I'm not naïve. Look at the timings."

"We've already figured that one out," Carlos replied.

"That's all for now, Mr Fish," Fiona said. "Stay in touch and help us find Princess."

After Travis left, Carlos remarked, "It's as we suspected. People are being paid to vandalise cameras and create distractions. While everyone thinks the riots are about looting or making political statements, it's really about providing cover for someone to eliminate loose ends."

Fiona nodded grimly. "What are your thoughts on our next move?"

"We need to uncover everything we can about Jodie Whitwick's investigation. You can use your authority to access the council offices on Monday. I'll reach out to her husband and Tony Hadden tomorrow. If Jodie had evidence regarding this grooming operation, they might not have found it. I'm also thinking about that fourth position at the clock tower."

"North-facing," Fiona said grimly. "Princess is going to die unless we can put a stop to this."

Carlos nodded. "We have to find Nicolae. He's the head of the snake. Cut him off, and perhaps we can save Princess if she's next on his list."

"What if we can't find him in time?"

"Then we flood the Foxdale Estate and the clock tower with police presence, making it impossible for anyone to be placed there without us knowing about it."

"That's going to require resources I don't have. But I'll speak to Superintendent Henley, if she'll listen. This is bigger than three murders; this is organised crime on a huge scale that's been operating under our noses for years."

"Let's call it a night. I'll make a fresh start in the morning," Carlos said.

"You go ahead. I want to ask Paul if he can contact Princess for us," Fiona replied. "I don't trust Travis Fish to risk his neck. In fact, I don't believe him at all."

"I'm with you on that one. We'll talk again tomorrow."

8

FIONA STOMPED FROM THE ANNEXE THROUGH THE church and into Paul's office, barging in without knocking. He looked up, that big attractive smile on his face, but she was in no mood.

"How do you deal with scumbags like Travis Fish? How can you even consider helping such people?"

Paul closed the Bible on his desk and met her gaze with his striking blue eyes. "I assume that's a rhetorical question, Fiona."

"No, it's not. I want to understand how you can allow men like him to mix with families and young girls. Who knows what he's doing behind your back. You realise he groomed women for a big shot, don't you?"

Fiona caught a flicker of shock in Paul's eyes. Fish hadn't been honest with him at all.

Paul composed himself and replied softly, "God allows all people into His church. While I understand you have a somewhat distorted view of the world, Travis is sorry for his past. He has put that life behind him and is now a changed man."

Fiona glared at him. "Yeah, well, if he's changed, which I'm not buying, he didn't do it soon enough, did he? Not for two of the dead women. I've got three bodies, and your convert has blood on his hands."

"I can see you're upset, Fiona. Can I make you a hot drink? Cocoa? Hot chocolate?"

Fiona wanted to tell him where to shove his hot drink, but instead, she sank into a chair, exhausted. "Hot chocolate would be good," she replied moodily.

Paul left her brooding in his office while he disappeared to prepare the drinks. It gave her time to process what she'd learned about Angela and Diane from Travis. Had Diane uncovered something that made her the actual target? The truth was that Fiona's anger about Nicolae's involvement gnawed at her. The fact that this grooming network had been operating for years right under their noses only worsened her mood. This Mr Cross bloke was most likely dead and buried or living a life of luxury on some Caribbean island. Of course she would try to track him down, but there wasn't much to go on. She would put the DCs on it. More resources wasted on people who didn't deserve it.

Paul returned and handed her a mug of hot chocolate before taking a seat in an armchair next to her.

Ever since she had met this man, Fiona had felt a powerful attraction to him. Not romantically, at least that's what she told herself. Deep down, she was angry with the world right now, but she admired what he did. He went out of his way to help people, even people like Travis Fish, who lived on a rundown estate. Paul was a good man, but men like Travis would let him down time and again. If only she could get to Nicolae. They sat in silence as she allowed the aroma of the hot chocolate to soothe her. Paul waited patiently, likely expecting her to vent some more.

When she didn't, he remarked, "I take it you learned some things tonight about your victims. Apart from being annoying, was it helpful?"

"Did Diamond and Angel ever tell you how they ended up on the street in the first place?"

Paul hesitated. "I've heard part of their story, but not all of it. When I met Angela, she didn't want to change, and neither did Diane. But Ruby's different; I can see she wants a way out. It's just difficult for them."

"You're mistaken about Angela and Diane," Fiona replied. "Both wanted out. Travis introduced them to a man who groomed them into addiction before persuading them to sell their bodies. Diane was off drugs but pretended to use them to avoid drawing attention to herself. She was searching for a way out, but you're right she didn't want God. The problem for her was that she wanted riches – her ex-husband told me and Carlos the same thing – she might have discovered something that got her killed. Angela might have been looking for a way out too, for all the good it did them."

"Feel free to use me as a sounding board," Paul offered. "Anything you say in this room, Fiona, will be treated in confidence, as long as you understand I won't discuss other people's pasts with you if they confide in me."

"Trust isn't high on my horizon," Fiona replied. "I think

I need to know a lot more about you to be convinced you're not involved."

Paul raised a bushy eyebrow but smiled that smile. "You don't believe that for one minute. I think your problem is that you're afraid to let anyone in."

Fiona flinched at his words. He was the first man she had met whom she believed could see right through her, and it terrified her. She broke eye contact. "How can you be sure Travis isn't playing you?"

"Nicely manoeuvred," Paul said. "I can't be certain, but I don't believe he is."

"Well, I'll tell you this for nothing, Pastor Allen: you've got a spy in your ranks. I believe someone in your congregation is reporting to a very dangerous man."

"I'm sorry if you don't like it, but I can't think that way, Fiona. If I start suspecting people in my congregation, I won't be able to function. How can I help people if I'suspect them?"

"Well, that's my job, isn't it?" Fiona replied with a reluctant grin. "In my line of work, you trust nobody and suspect everybody."

"That must lead to a very lonely life, Fiona."

Every time he said her name, an electric current shot through her heart, and it frightened her. "I do all right," she said, taking a sip of hot chocolate. "Jacobi is a friend. I trust him."

"At least that's something," Paul said thoughtfully.

Fiona no longer looked at him; she didn't dare. Paul Allen's searching gaze intimidated her. He made her want to run away and hide like a silly schoolgirl. And that was exactly how she was behaving right now, like a petulant teenager. "Anyway, the reason I'm here is to ask you what you can tell me about Princess," she said.

Paul leaned back in his chair, which groaned under his weight. He was a big, hefty man. She wondered what had led him to become a minister. He wasn't your typical preachy type. The vicar at her church was in his sixties, upper crust, and could do with a decent meal. But that vicar was sincere and a safe pair of hands. People in her congregation liked him. Not that she'd been to a service for a while. Her work demanded too much of her these days. When she had a Sunday off, all she wanted to do was spend the morning in bed.

"Why are you asking about Princess?" Paul's question broke through her thoughts, carving the atmosphere in two.

"You probably realise already, but she was in contact with both Ruby and Angela. I think you were there when Ruby said she'd broken away from their, erm, support group."

"Yes, I was there when Ruby said that. Princess is vulnerable but cold," Paul replied. "I can't penetrate her barriers, so I don't know what goes on in her mind. It seems to me she's longing for something she once had."

"Mr Cross," Fiona snapped, dripping with cynicism. "The man responsible for getting women hooked on drugs and doing his bidding."

"I'm not familiar with a Mr Cross," Paul said.

"They don't tell you everything, do they? If it's any consolation, I doubt that's his real name," Fiona said. "He's missing but might have been a member of your congregation. Has anyone gone missing in the last year?"

"People come and go on the estate, mostly because they move up the housing ladder when they can afford somewhere with better schools. There are no guarantees, of course. Angela went to one of those 'excellent' schools."

"Are you certain you've never heard of Mr Cross?"

Paul looked at her. "Tell me about him."

"Travis can tell you more than I can. I only have what he told me, and he reckons they never met. He was a businessman who paid people like Travis for introductions. Then Cross groomed the young women, got them addicted to drugs, placed a few in flats, and persuaded them to go on the game. My guess is that he was nothing more than an upper-class pimp, taking a large cut of their earnings."

"If you're trying to shock me, it's not working. I understand what happens unless they are picked up as homeless. I also know that women are trafficked from abroad. To be honest, I've noticed a lot of that lately."

"And yet you don't report it," Fiona said cynically. "I can't ask you to spy for me, Paul, but if you hear anything, particularly regarding a Romanian man, please contact me."

"People need to be able to confide in me, Fiona. That's how it works here. If I lose their trust, I'll lose half the congregation and all that we've worked hard to establish. We still face attacks on the church, but mostly, I've developed an uneasy relationship with these people. I have agreements in place that nobody comes after the girls who choose a different lifestyle. If I report to you... In fact, if I'm seen with you too often, it will send the wrong message."

"I'm not asking you to tell me everything, Paul, but the man I'm after is truly dangerous. If I shared half of what I know about him, you'd be eager to help me. And don't think for one minute he's got a conscience. He won't end up being one of your lost sheep."

"I have to believe that anyone can change, Fiona." He raised his hand to stop her from interrupting. "But I hear you. If I come across anything I feel I can share, I will. But please, don't come here too often."

"It's a bit late for that," said Fiona. "I need you to arrange a meeting with Princess."

"In that case, we'd better conduct any discussions like this when there's nobody around. Not after public meetings. I make no promises, but I'll try to arrange a meeting when we're closed and have no activities going on. And please don't come in your car, as they'll recognise it."

"Okay, I understand. We wouldn't want to put you in danger anyway. I don't want the man we're after to think for one moment that you might snitch on him. I'm fairly certain Jodie Whitwick had something on him."

"The anti-prostitution councillor?"

"Yes," Fiona replied. "She had been doing a lot of digging. Her offices were ransacked on the night of one of the riots, as was her home office. These men were clearly looking for whatever evidence she had. I'm not sure if they found it, but she ended up dead."

"And if they found nothing, why would they kill her?"

"Precautionary," Fiona replied. "Or perhaps as a warning to others not to investigate. I suspect it all began when Angela upset our man's applecart. I don't think they intended to place girls around the clock tower. However, having done the first one, and after the press interpreted it as the work of some sort of religious fanatic, the man at the top seized the opportunity. From then on, he created the impression that a vigilante religious figure was responsible for the killings. He uses distraction to create havoc on the streets while he does away with any threats to his organisation."

"Can't you just arrest him?"

"I wouldn't know where to begin. Every time we get close, he slips away. He's as slippery as an eel. We had him once, and somehow, he still got away, then left the country. While he was gone, all our evidence against him disappeared. Now I believe he's back, but not only do we have no idea where to find him, we also lack the evidence to put him away. I'm hoping that Jodie Whitwick's family, friends, or colleagues might help us find what she knew. But it's a long shot because they'll be terrified now, and I can't imagine they haven't been warned off." Fiona didn't mention the fact that Diane may have also possessed evidence that got her killed.

Paul stroked his bushy beard. "This guy does sound dangerous. What's his name?"

"I will not give you a name," Fiona said, "because if you mention it and a spy in your congregation hears you, I don't want what happens to you on my conscience."

"Fair enough," Paul replied. "You've given me a lot to think about, Fiona, but I need to carry out God's work without fear. That's my calling."

"One day, I'm going to ask you how you got that calling," Fiona said. "But right now, it's been a long day and I'm extremely tired. I expect you are too."

"I'll be here for a few more hours yet. I've got a sermon to prepare for tomorrow," said Paul. "But you go home and rest, Fiona. It's been nice talking to you." He stood up at the same time she did. She wasn't small, but she only came to chest height on him.

"Are you sure you're not an all-in wrestler pretending to be a Baptist minister?"

Paul laughed a deep, throaty laugh. "I could say something in return," he said, looking at her.

She imagined what that might be: she was scruffy, and he probably thought she could be a bag lady in another life. "But you're too much of a gentleman."

"Something like that. I really was sorry to hear about your father, Fiona. If you need bereavement counselling or just a listening ear, we could meet elsewhere."

She held both palms up. "On that note, I'll say goodnight."

She hurried out of the church and climbed into her Mini, feeling foolish but too exhausted to dwell on it. Paul stood at the door, waving her off, and she watched him fade from view in her rearview mirror.

9

Tony Hadden had been feeling smug since his two-page spread had been printed in the local paper the night before. He had dedicated a considerable amount of time piecing together the events leading up to the murders of three women and even more investigating the life and achievements of Councillor Jodie Whitwick.

Today, he treated himself to lunch at his favourite restaurant in Stoney Stanton and visited his mother in Earl Shilton. The only dampener was that his mother's health had been failing since his father's death. Tony tried to put that out of his mind as he poured himself a large brandy. He studied the open newspaper spread out on an antique coffee table. His love for antiques cost him a fortune, but he could afford them.

Before going freelance, Tony had been an ambitious reporter for the Leicester Mercury. When his car had been deliberately forced off the road while he was following a lead

– for his own career and for a case Carlos had been working on – he had survived only to receive a visit in hospital from a man with a deadly message. It was simple. Keep your mouth shut. Shortly before the incident on that fateful night, Tony had called Carlos to tell him he had important information. He never got the chance to share it because his car was forced into a ditch.

Not satisfied with the result, a man had tried to make sure Tony didn't survive by pouring an accelerant over the car and setting it alight. Thankfully, he hadn't checked to see if Tony was inside; otherwise, he wouldn't be alive today. The accident that was not an accident led to him being rushed to a special burns' unit in Nottingham, followed by extensive rehabilitation. He still bore scars on his face and torso, although they weren't as severe as they could have been because he had escaped. What didn't heal were the internal scars.

When he regained consciousness after the accident, he received the visit. The man made it clear what would happen to him and his parents if he disclosed what he knew to Carlos. Tony had been a coward, but Jodie Whitwick was no coward. She had confronted dangerous men, one of whom he was convinced had been behind his brush with death, and she had paid the ultimate price. At least he could highlight her heroism. Tony couldn't uncover why the other two women had been murdered, but he suspected it was because they knew too much or they had been decoys, with the plan being to kill Jodie Whitwick all along. He was sure Carlos would take that into consideration.

Tony still debated whether he should tell Carlos what he had discovered about the man Nicolae. The man who had visited the hospital took his phone SIM and tablet, but Tony was always careful about his sources and had already downloaded the information to a secure cloud that only he knew about.

As the warmth of the brandy settled in his stomach, it gave him courage. Maybe now was the time. But could he risk it? Was the major player still out there? He had gone away, but with all that was happening in the city at the moment, Tony had a nasty suspicion he was back. And back with a vengeance.

Tony liked Carlos. He even liked the DI who Carlos sometimes partnered, but the risk to himself, and more importantly, to his mother, the only person he had left in the world, would be astronomical. He was now a senior freelance journalist with the freedom to pursue stories that paid well, and he wanted to maintain that position. Those harrowing days in intensive care, and the fact that he had been fortunate to walk away from that blazing car, had shown just how fleeting life could be. He still suffered daily pain and endured nightmares and flashbacks. Challenging the status quo at this point wouldn't be the thing to do; that was Carlos's job. And the DI's. Tony wasn't a brave man. His job was to write stories the public wanted to read. And tonight was a night for celebration, not reminiscing.

As he sat in his favourite armchair, a second glass of brandy in hand, he reflected on the man he had become. Celebration for a newspaper man or woman usually meant tragedy for someone else. In the article he took such pride in, he had highlighted three tragedies that needed thorough investigation: three deaths, injured police officers, and a developing inquiry. Tony's job wasn't to develop a conscience; it was to sell newspapers. He could not afford to mourn the deaths of others, though he sometimes felt sad about the waste of life. The day he grew too much of a conscience would be the day he needed to pack it all in. He had built up a decent pension pot now, so he could retire at any time. But while he enjoyed the thrill of seeing his stories in print, he would continue.

Before being run off the road, Tony had been like a terrier, chomping at the heels of any story. His ambition had been to work for one of the bigger national papers. But nobody knew better than he did that when he was discharged from hospital, he was a shell of the man he'd been before. Now, he had settled for a magnificent house in a pleasant suburb. He drove a statement car and was a respected journalist who didn't need to be tied to one newspaper. Life was good.

So why was this Nicolae thing still eating at him? It was because, as a newspaperman, he wanted to tell the story, and he hated being threatened. Tony's landline rang, pulling him from his musings. He answered, but there was silence at the other end. "Hello?" The caller hung up.

Tony shook his head, not recognising the number on the caller display screen. Probably a sales call. The phone rang again. He lifted the receiver. "Hello?" Still no reply. "Look, whoever this is, if you're selling, I'm not buying, and if you've got a story, contact my desk." Tony often received calls with tip-offs, but not usually on his landline. The only calls he got on his landline were from his mother, his ex-wife, or someone trying to sell him insurance.

An uncomfortable thought crossed his mind. Had the story rattled someone's cage? His heart sank. Maybe he had no choice but to tell Carlos now. Was he in danger? He tried to shrug it off, taking another large swig of brandy and putting the phone down, unplugging it from the wall. He wasn't going down that route.

Tony polished off the final dregs of brandy, and his mobile rang. Carlos's name flashed up on the screen.

"Hello Carlos, I was just thinking about you."

"Hi Tony, I was wondering if we could meet for lunch tomorrow. I haven't had a chance to read through what you told Julie yesterday, but I'm on my way back to the office now."

"Are you driving?"

"Yes, but you're on hands-free, so can you make lunch tomorrow?"

"Would you mind coming over?"

"What now?" Carlos asked.

"Yeah, we need to talk."

"Are you still at the office?"

"No, I'm at home."

"Fine, text me the address, and I'll see you soon. Do you want to tell me what this is about?"

"Not over the phone," said Tony, ending the call. He texted his address and placed his mobile next to him. His hands were trembling. It's time. He couldn't let them intimidate him again. He would arrange for his mother to be moved into a good care home. They had been discussing it for a long time, and Tony still had enough contacts to make her disappear off anyone's radar. At least he hoped he did. He needed this off his chest, and then if they wanted to come after him, well...

He wandered over to the window and looked outside. The security gates were closed, but he pressed the button to open them for Carlos's arrival. Security cameras surrounded the property. He had installed them when he bought the place. He checked the large monitor with a live feed from all around the house. Nothing. Maybe the call that spooked him was a prank. Either way, he would speak to Carlos while he had the courage.

After pouring himself another brandy, he noticed one of his cameras flickering before going dark. He hadn't been watching the driveway but didn't think anyone had driven in. Sometimes there were glitches with him being in the sticks, but his heart thumped against his chest as he fiddled with the lead. Another camera went dark, but Tony still couldn't see anyone. He dialled 999 and asked for the police.

"There's an intruder about to break into my house. They're outside now. Come quickly." Tony had to answer a few tedious questions before giving his address.

"Can you stay on the phone, sir?"

Tony put the phone on speaker as another camera went dark. Just one left. "Hurry, they're cutting off my surveillance system."

"There's a car on the way, sir," said the dispatcher.

"Well, tell them to hurry." Tony ended the call, wishing he hadn't unplugged the landline, and called Carlos.

"Almost there, Tony."

"I think it might be too late now, Carlos." Tony tried to sound calm. "Let's do this another time."

"Are you sure?" Carlos sounded confused. "I'm about five minutes out."

"Best if we do it another time. We'll do lunch tomorrow." Tony ended the call. If they were going to get him, he would not deliver Carlos into their hands at the same time. Tony went to his desk and fired up his desktop computer. He brought up the hidden folder and attached it to an email. It was an email he knew he would one day have to send. At least this time, the guy would go down. But the lights went out, and his Wi-Fi went dead.

Tony heard the front door open. Whoever it was, they were professionals. So much for state-of-the-art security. Footsteps crossed the parquet floor he'd spent so much money on.

He looked up when a torch shone in his face. He could make out three shadows in the darkness. Tony tried to smile.

"Take whatever you like, guys. I keep little of value in the house. Just take what you can find." He waved his arms nonchalantly, but the tremor in his voice betrayed him.

A hood covered his head, and everything went black as rough arms dragged him out of the house.

"Make sure that surveillance is back up as soon as we leave and doctor the timeframe before the cops get here. I'm sure he called them."

"Yes, boss."

"And don't forget to lock up. Put a message on his answering machine with a lead to a story in London and bring his car with you."

That was the only conversation Tony overheard before the car door closed and the men took off. He was shaking so hard his ribs ached; if only he didn't live in the country, the police would have arrived in time to save him. He closed his eyes, trying to accept the inevitable.

10

Carlos pulled into his private car park, still mulling over why Tony had invited him over tonight and then changed his mind. If he weren't so tired, he would go now, but if Tony said it could wait until tomorrow, he would accept that. The weight of exhaustion pressed down on his shoulders like a heavy barbell. His day hadn't been long, but after staying up to call Rachel and then going over the case in his mind – a whirlwind of half-formed theories and unanswered questions – it felt longer. He had forgotten to check what Julie had discovered when he collected Lady from the office the night before and had stayed home to carry out background checks on the deceased women.

Tony's article had been thorough, but he needed to warn him not to hint that Angel and Diamond's deaths were decoys. His reporter friend didn't realise Nicolae was back, otherwise he would have been more circumspect. Carlos decided to call Tony when he got into his office to warn him to be on his guard.

So many options spun around in his mind since the conversation with Travis Fish, each leading to more possibilities. He didn't trust Fish any more than Fiona did, but right now, he just wanted to get into his office, make notes, and try to piece together what they had learned. That was how he processed things – writing it down and watching connections emerge on paper.

As he switched off the engine, the familiar tick-tick of the cooling motor filled the silence. Lady sat bolt upright in the passenger seat, her body rigid. A low growl rumbled deep in her throat, barely audible but unmistakable.

"What's up, girl?" Carlos reached over to stroke her head, but she didn't relax. Her eyes were fixed on something in the darkness beyond the windscreen. Carlos was already opening the driver's side door when he realised something was wrong. The security light hadn't lit up.

Sensing danger, he tried to pull the door closed, but a boot jammed the gap, stopping it with a heavy thud and a man cursing. Carlos was now fully alert, but a bright light shone directly in his eyes, blinding him. White spots danced in his vision as he blinked the light away. He couldn't see a thing.

Hands roughly pulled him from the vehicle; at least four hands were grabbing at his jacket, arms, and collar. Carlos twisted hard, trying to escape. He drove an elbow into someone's ribs, feeling the solid connection and hearing the same man whose foot got crushed curse. The sharp expletive cut through the night, but there were too many of them. More hands and arms pinned him tight, pressing him down. He couldn't move his arms. His shoulders burned with the strain of trying to break free.

Carlos couldn't move anything but his legs, so he kicked backwards, driving his heel into what he hoped was a shin. It connected with bone, causing another man to swear. It was too dark to see his attackers, who wore hoods over their faces. Their bodies were mere shadows against the darkness, but he could feel them. At least four, maybe five. Too many.

He was slammed down onto the old tarmac, the rough surface scraping his cheek. A knee pressed into his back, making him gasp for air. He tried to wriggle his hands free, twisting his wrists, but the grip on him was iron-strong. Then a boot kicked his head, resulting in a sharp pain. Stars exploded in his vision.

"Enough!" someone shouted. The voice had authority that the others responded to. "Tie him up," came the command.

Carlos's hands were wrenched behind his back, plastic cable ties biting into his wrists. His ankles were bound next, the ties so tight they almost cut off his circulation. Lady was barking frantically, a desperate, high-pitched sound that tore at his heart. He could hear her throwing herself against her safety harness, trying to free herself. Part of him hoped she wouldn't get loose; another part hoped she'd somehow break free and run for help. Deep down, he knew she wouldn't leave him, and these men would kill her without a second thought.

Carlos was dragged roughly to his feet. Then came the punches – one to his face, where he felt blood streaming from his lip. Another to his abdomen, driving deep into his solar plexus. He couldn't breathe, couldn't think; he could only endure blow after blow. Finally, they stopped. One of the men leaned down, his face hidden by a black balaclava with only his eyes visible through holes – cold eyes. He growled, his breath hot and sour on Carlos's pained face.

"Take this as a warning."

Carlos spat blood on the ground. His lip swelling rapidly, he could barely form words, but he managed somehow. "A warning against what?" He could taste the metallic, coppery blood in his mouth. He'd had worse in the army, much worse, and was well able to withstand pain. But it didn't make it any easier.

"To mind your own business." The balaclava muffled the man's voice, disguising it, but Carlos detected a Leicester accent. "Cut all ties with the detective."

Carlos stared at the man, memorising what little he could see. The shape of his head, round. The set of his shoulders. "That's not going to happen," he said defiantly.

Another fist pummelled into Carlos's ribs, and this time he heard it crack. The pain was immediate and searing, like a hot knife sliding between his bones. He gasped, doubling over as much as his bound hands and the men holding him would allow.

"Be it on your head then."

The leader allowed the others to throw a few more punches while Lady was going demented, trapped in the front seat by the tether meant to protect her. Her barks turned to howls, desperate to reach him. Carlos tried to call to her, to calm her, but he couldn't find enough air in his lungs.

Then the lead man yelled. “Get the dog!”

“No. No, you don’t need to do that.” Pure terror flooded Carlos’s veins as he forced the words out. “This is between your employers and me. Leave—“

His words were cut off as Lady yelped. The sound went through him like a physical blow, worse than any punch they had landed. The next thing he saw was his dog, muzzled, fighting to reach him. She was straining against a lead the men had put on her, her eyes wild and fearful.

“No!” Carlos’s voice cracked. “Please!”

“Next time it will be you,” the man said, his voice flat, emotionless. “Or maybe even your wife. Our reach is long, Mr Jacobi. Very long.”

Carlos felt his heart was about to burst. Tears blinded him, hot and humiliating, streaming down his face. “Please,” he pleaded, all pride gone, all pretence of strength abandoned. “Leave the dog. Take me. Do whatever you want to me but leave her alone.”

The man’s laugh was cruel, hollow almost, a sound without warmth or humanity. “If you care this much about a dog, just imagine what we can do to your wife. Think about that. Think about what might happen to her if you keep sticking your nose where it doesn’t belong.”

Carlos struggled with every ounce of energy left in his body, bursting every sinew, straining until something tore in his shoulder. He didn’t care. He had to get free, had to stop them from taking Lady. But the ties held firm, cutting deeper into his wrists.

He watched helplessly as two of the men dragged Lady away. She was fighting them every step, digging her paws into the ground, trying to pull back towards him. Her muffled whines cut through his heart like razors.

The leader and another man turned to Carlos's beloved Capri. He had restored it himself over the years, spending hundreds of hours on it. He watched, numb, as one of them lifted a brick from the ground. The man hurled it through the front window. Glass exploded, glittering shards flying everywhere. But even that was nothing compared to the pain of hearing Lady's whines through the muzzle.

The men turned to leave, their footsteps receding into the darkness. Carlos could still hear Lady. "I'm begging you," he called, his voice breaking. "Let my dog go. Please."

The only response was the evil cackle of the men as they disappeared. Anger replaced the pain. What he would do to these men if he could only free himself. But wrestle as he might, he remained tethered.

He was left in silence. A deep profound silence, broken only by his ragged breathing.

Fiona's ringtone burst through the night. He could see the flashing screen from under the front wheel of his car but couldn't reach it. He closed his eyes, fresh tears streaming down his face. Lady. *They've got Lady.*

11

Fiona pulled up her Mini at the marina entrance and parked in her designated space. She sat for a moment to stare into the dark night before hauling her tired body out of the car. Every movement was an effort. For weeks, her heart had ached from the loss of her father, a dull but constant pain that wouldn't go away. The murder case provided a significant distraction from her grief, at least it had until Paul's sympathetic gaze brought it rushing back. She hesitated to discuss her feelings with him, fearing her mask would crack. At times, she felt on the verge of breaking, and his well-meaning interference only intensified her struggle.

Shaking off her depressing thoughts, Fiona focused instead on the young women being manipulated and forced into prostitution by this Mr Cross, two of whom were now dead. That was troubling enough, but the realisation that Nicolae had likely been the mastermind all along ignited a fury within her that was difficult to contain. Carlos had been right about Nicolae from the word go. She wished she'd got him when she had the chance, instead succumbing to emotional blackmail from the dodgy lawyer in Edinburgh. At least he was behind bars. This time, Nicolae would not escape. He had ruined lives, taken too many lives, and shattered too many families. With Carlos's help, she was determined to put him away, no matter the cost.

As she pulled her raincoat collar up as a buffer against the chill coming off the River Soar and began walking along the towpath, she noticed her new neighbours approaching. The hippy couple in their early thirties, who always wore mismatched patchwork colours, had moved onto the boat three spaces down from hers two months earlier. Their tie-dye coats brightened the night. They possessed that glazed look typical of those who spent most of their time stoned, something Fiona preferred to ignore. They rarely engaged with their boating neighbours, aside from casual greetings, which suited Fiona just fine. She had enough complications in her life without adding drama with neighbours to the mix. Thus, she was taken aback when they called out to her.

"Fiona?"

She stopped, impatiently trying to remember if they had ever exchanged names. As far as she could recall, they hadn't. Why choose this night of all nights to stop and chat? Fiona had reports to write and Nicolae to pursue.

"Hello," she replied, striving to keep irritation from her voice.

As they reached her, the woman smiled a dreamy, unfocused smile. Her long hair appeared to be greying at the temples – perhaps she was older than Fiona had initially thought. The hair hung in loose waves, partially obscuring her face.

"Your brother said to tell you he's waiting for you."

A chill sensation ran down Fiona's spine. "Where is he?"

"On your boat." The woman gestured vaguely in the direction of Fiona's mooring, her hand moving in languid arcs through the air.

"Thanks."

Heart racing, Fiona broke into a run, her feet pounding the towpath. If her brother was here, he was in trouble. Her boat was a fair distance from the entrance, as she had been among the last to secure a mooring until the couple took over from a man who had gone into hospital and never returned. They must have inherited the boat, as the marina had been full when she applied, and she had waited nearly six months for a space. Her running was stop-start because of her lack of fitness. She cursed herself for being overweight, a concern that rarely bothered her, but the comfort-eating following her father's death had taken its toll. When had she last taken any exercise that was not work-related? Years was the answer.

The towpath curved ahead, lined with familiar houseboats, most of their windows dark at this hour. A few had lights on, their inhabitants living normal lives. She ran past them all, breath coming in harsh gasps, her side cramping. She had to keep stopping, bending over to catch her breath before continuing. A brisk walk would have got her there faster, but she wasn't thinking straight.

When she finally reached her boat, it was shrouded in darkness. There was no movement outside. Nothing but the gentle lapping of the river against her old, decrepit home.

"Steve?" she called, but there was no reply.

She paused at the side of her mooring, hands on her knees, trying to catch her breath and cursing the couple for playing jokes on her. They must have discovered she was a detective and decided to have some fun at her expense. If they wanted to play games, their pot-smoking days were over. But how would they know she had a brother? Just then, a whiff of petrol hung in the night breeze – every boat owner's nightmare. The strong, pungent odour made her eyes water.

Fiona stepped back just in time as the boat erupted into an inferno. It happened so quickly; one moment there was darkness, and the next, an explosion of orange and red flames shot from the deck, engulfing the longboat in seconds. Though every instinct urged her to run towards her beloved home, the heat forced her back another step. She stood frozen as the windows shattered with a loud crack.

"Steve? Please God. No!" she cried, summoning enough courage to run forward. She had to climb aboard and find her baby brother. She had promised her mother years ago, and her father as he lay dying, that she would always protect him. Suddenly, powerful arms wrapped around her from behind, pinning her own arms to her sides. She struggled, imagining it was a neighbour trying to prevent her from doing something reckless. "Let me go! I have to save my brother!"

When she turned her head, she saw the man was wearing a balaclava, the black fabric obscuring his face.

"Take this as a warning," he hissed in her ear, the smell of cigarettes on his breath mixing with cheap aftershave. Before she could react, he disappeared. Fiona heard his footsteps retreating along the towpath, but her trembling legs and pounding heart wouldn't allow her to pursue him.

Her neighbours emerged from their boats, armed with fire extinguishers. Someone was reeling in the fire hose from the marina's emergency fire point. People shouted, coordinating their efforts, but Fiona remained frozen, watching her home burn to ash. Flames leapt twenty feet high, consuming everything. People were told to stand back while a brave soul had the foresight to disconnect her gas canisters and move them away from the scene before they could explode. It was like watching a film in slow motion but she was powerless to do anything.

Her refuge, her sanctuary, was being consumed. Someone called for the fire brigade and the police, shouting the address into his phone.

She pulled out her own phone, hands shaking as she dialled her brother's number.

"Hi, Sis, how are you?" Steve's cheerful voice came through, accompanied by music and laughter in the background.

"Where are you?" Fiona gasped, struggling to control the tremor in her voice. She flopped down on the grassy verge, relief flooding through her.

"Just got home. It's one of the guys I work with's birthday. We went for drinks after work and have come back here to watch a film. Are you okay, Fiona? You sound weird."

She wanted to bury her head in the long grass and sob.

Steve wasn't on the boat. "I'm fine. Just thinking about you, that's all."

"Are you missing him?"

"Sorry, Steve, it's good to hear your voice, but I've got to go." She hung up before he could ask any more questions or before she fell apart.

Fiona pulled herself to her feet, watching as the fire brigade arrived and a police constable cordoned off the area. Dazed, she saw her home burn down to the waterline. The flames were dying down, having consumed most of what was combustible. At least her neighbours had prevented the fire from spreading to other boats, and no-one had been harmed.

Fiona pulled her raincoat tighter around herself, feeling suddenly cold now that the flames had died down. Her next-door neighbour cast her a sympathetic look but was pushed back by fire officers determined to prevent anyone from getting burned. A female police officer Fiona recognised approached her.

"Are you okay, Ma'am?"

Fiona nodded.

"Is it convenient to take a statement?"

Fiona wasn't listening, her mind was elsewhere. Carlos! She thought. I need to warn Carlos.

She told the officer to give her a minute and to interview her neighbours first to see if they had witnessed anything. Fiona dialled Carlos's number, but it rang until his voicemail cut in.

"Carlos, it's Fiona. Call me back as soon as you hear this. Be careful," she added.

As she watched the smoke drift away on the night breeze,

the charred remains of her home sinking lower into the water with only a few remnants floating away on the tide, Fiona felt a determination settle over her. They'd made a mistake tonight. *If they think they can scare me again or warn me off, they are mistaken. All they've done is make it personal.*

Nicolae and whoever he was working with had just declared war, and Fiona Cook had never backed down from a fight in her life. She wasn't about to start now. She waved to the officer as she staggered towards the towpath. "I'll give you my statement as soon as I've called the CSI team."

"We can do that." A fire officer approached her. "We can see this wasn't an accident."

"Thanks," said Fiona as she walked away from the scene.

"Where are you going, Ma'am?"

Not leaving the officer any choice but to follow, Fiona headed along the towpath the way she'd come. She wanted to have a word with her hippy neighbours and knew exactly where they would be.

"There's a pub at the marina; you can interview me there. I need a hot drink."

12

After a lecture on walking home from the hospital in the early hours, Gary encouraged Sara to talk over dinner about her experience of finding the body at the clock tower. He was aware of the investigation into the mysterious deaths and complained about working with a woman he described as an arrogant DC, interviewing people on the Foxdale Estate. Gary listened intently as Sara recounted her interview with the private investigator, Carlos Jacobi, wanting every detail until she pointed out that his interest was sounding like another interview. "I just want to put the whole thing behind me," she said.

"In that case, let me buy you another glass of wine," Gary offered.

The evening turned out to be much better than she had expected. It was the first chance to meet her partner since that night at the hospital. Having dinner at the Holiday Inn Hotel after Gary finished his shift was certainly a boredom buster even if she didn't understand why he was so eager to buy her dinner. Gary was in a stable relationship, and Sara had never received any signals that his interest in her extended beyond that of a work partner. She attributed his behaviour to being like an overprotective older brother, not to mention an inquisitive officer.

Once the serious conversation was over, Gary made her laugh with terrible impressions of their sergeant, and for a few hours, she could forget about the stitches in her head, the night terrors that had haunted her every night since the attack, and that she suspected she wasn't trusted to return to duty.

When the meal was finished, Sara and Gary left the hotel arm in arm. It wasn't often she drank wine, and her head was spinning slightly from the two large glasses Gary had poured for her. She was grateful not to be taking painkillers anymore, as the combination would have been overwhelming. The cold air hit her face as soon as they emerged from the warm lobby, helping to dispel the effects of the alcohol.

"When do you think you'll be back at work?" Gary asked as they strolled away from the hotel. "This DC Maplin they've lumbered me with thinks she's my boss."

Sara sighed. "I don't know when I'll be back." And that was the truth. She had debated with herself all evening whether she should tell Gary she was considering leaving the force. She even rehearsed the conversation and his inevitable counterarguments in her head, but she couldn't find the words. He'd been so happy to see her, his face lighting up when she walked into the restaurant, and the fact that he was struggling with the DC from DI Cook's team made it even harder. Moreover, she loved her job and wasn't sure if her decision was about her or her mother. Her mind was as conflicted as ever, and she didn't want to make a rash decision based on one incident. Maybe she could still make a difference.

"Do you want a lift up the High Street?" Gary asked, taking car keys out of his pocket.

Sara furrowed her brows after witnessing him down three pints of lager. "Don't you think you should take a taxi?"

"Come on, Sara, live a little. Who's going to arrest me?"

Sara found the arrogance of certain police officers who believed they were above the law disturbing. She glared at him. "You're over the limit, Gary."

He rubbed the back of his neck, frowning, but then grinned. "It's just that I still don't like you walking out alone at this time of night. Especially after... you know."

"I'll be fine," she said, trying to sound confident. The truth was, the flashbacks from the attack weren't easing, but she would not give in to them. If she let fear control her, she might as well quit right now. "It's a ten-minute walk, tops. But I'll call you a cab if you like."

"You win," Gary's laugh sounded forced. They had been partners long enough for him to read her. "I'll call someone from my car." He headed for his car, which was parked on double yellows outside the hotel entrance. "One of the perks of the job," he had said with a wink when they met up. Sara was never comfortable bending the rules, even small ones, and especially not when the car park fees were extortionate.

"Do you want me to park that in the car park for you?" Sara asked.

"I'll call a mate to drive it, and me, home."

"Okay, catch you soon." Sara turned towards the High Street before stopping in her tracks. "What's that sound?"

"What?" Gary paused, his hand on the door handle.

They both listened. For a moment, the only sounds were the familiar noises of the city: traffic on the ring road, the bass thump of music from a club, and a car alarm wailing in the distance. Then Sara heard it again. A scuffle accompanied by the sound of something being dragged along the pavement, followed by a heart-wrenching whine. It came from across the road. Sara was on the move subconsciously reacting to her instincts overriding common sense. A car screeched to a halt, and she saw two men hurrying towards it. One man was dragging something behind him. A dog that twisted and fought, straining against the leash, a muzzle on its face.

"There's a dog!" Sara shouted. "I recognise that dog!"

As she drew closer, she could see clearly. The tan and white springer spaniel she had met when Carlos interviewed her. The beautiful dog he had with him when they met at the clock tower.

"Lady?" she called. "Hey! Stop! Police!" Sara shouted, infusing her voice with every ounce of authority she could muster.

The men spun around, startled. In their surprise, the man holding the lead must have loosened his grip. Lady wrenched free and bolted as if she had a mission too important to miss. Her paws skittered along the pavement as she ran. The men jumped into a dark SUV. Sara noticed the number plate was covered as it sped away, tyres squealing in protest.

"Lady! Wait!" Sara called, but the dog was already disappearing up the High Street.

Gary pulled up next to her, the engine running. "No time to argue. Climb in," he said. "We can go after them."

"No. Call for help, Gary." Sara's eyes remained fixed on the direction Lady had taken. "Carlos Jacobi must be in trouble. That's his dog." Her mind raced. "We need to follow her."

Sara started running, following the direction the dog had taken. Gary quickly reversed and overtook her, pulling up outside an office building where he got on his phone. Sara caught up, breathing hard, and noticed the sign on the door: Jacobi Investigations. But Lady wasn't at the front entrance; she had continued on, disappearing down a side road that ran behind the building. Gary was out of the car, following Sara as she sprinted after the dog.

"Where's it gone?" he asked.

"There must be a car park at the back," Sara replied, already turning down the narrow road. "Hear that?"

Delighted whines, high-pitched and frantic, reached her ears, along with Carlos's voice, sounding devastated yet happy at the same time.

When they entered the car park, darkness enveloped them. Gary shone a torch, revealing Carlos on the ground, his hands and ankles bound with cable ties, his face a mess of blood and swelling. The car, which Sara assumed belonged to him, had a smashed windscreen. Meanwhile, Lady was frantically trying to bite through the ties, her muzzle still on, whining and pawing at Carlos.

"Don't worry, girl," Sara said gently, kneeling beside the dog. She carefully removed the muzzle and stroked Lady's head. "I admire your determination but let me handle this."

Lady licked her hand gratefully before immediately returning to nuzzle Carlos with her nose.

Gary was back on his phone, requesting an ambulance. His voice sounded professional as he gave their location and described their findings. "I've already called for backup, but he needs the paramedics. I'll head out to the High Street and wait for them."

Sara wondered if Gary was going to suck on some mints to mask the fact that he had been drinking, but he wasn't her concern at that moment. She reached into her handbag, which she had placed on the ground. She always kept a Swiss Army knife inside it ever since she had been unable to cut someone from a seatbelt after being the first on scene of a car crash. Carefully, she cut through the cable ties that had dug painfully into Carlos's wrists, leaving angry red marks on both his wrists and ankles. Tears streamed down the private investigator's face as he embraced his dog.

"I thought she was dead," he said, his voice cracking. "I thought they'd killed her."

"They didn't," Sara replied, moving to his ankles to cut through the remaining ties. "She's okay now."

"How did you find her?" Carlos held his dog tightly, grimacing with pain and relief. Lady made small sounds of distress, sensing his discomfort.

"Let's remove these, and I'll explain." Sara cut through

the last tie and helped him sit up properly. He winced, one hand going to his ribs. Just then, a phone rang.

"It's Fiona's ringtone," Carlos said immediately. "She's tried a few times. I think she might be in trouble."

Sara glanced around, following the sound, and spotted the flashing light. She found the phone half-hidden under the front wheel of his car. The screen was cracked, but it was still functional. She handed it to him, and he placed it on speaker with shaking hands.

"Carlos? Thank God," the DI's voice sounded stressed. "I need to warn you."

"Too late, Fiona," Carlos's voice was steadier now. "But I'm okay. I'm with PCs Ransom and Hodge. They saved Lady's life. I couldn't warn you because I was tied up. Are you okay?"

"I am, but my boat is toast. They set fire to it, Carlos. Some guy in a balaclava gave me a warning."

"Yeah, me too." Carlos eyed Sara, and she noticed a calculating expression in his eyes. He was processing what had happened.

Gary returned with two paramedics, a man and a woman clad in green uniforms, both carrying equipment bags. The woman knelt beside Carlos, prompting Sara to step back and allow her to assess his injuries.

"Ma'am," Sara said into the phone, "Carlos is badly injured. He needs to go to the hospital."

"Understood," Fiona replied.

"I'm not going without Lady," Carlos stated flatly as the female paramedic reached for his arm to check his pulse. His dog was nestled against his legs, as if glued to him, trembling slightly but refusing to move. "I won't leave her."

"I'm sorry, sir, but we can't take a dog in the ambulance," the wiry male paramedic said, his world-weary eyes suggesting he had seen it all. However, his voice remained kind. "Regulations."

"Then treat me here," Carlos insisted. It wasn't a request; Lady whined and pressed closer to him as the paramedics attempted to examine him around her.

The paramedics exchanged glances. "What do we do? We can't force him into the ambulance."

Fiona's tired but understanding laugh came through the phone's speaker. "You won't separate him from his dog. Do as he says. Treat him there. But PC Ransom... Sara, stay with him until I arrive. I'll finish up here and meet you at your office, Carlos."

"Sorry about your boat, Fiona," Carlos said, and Sara recognised the genuine regret in his voice.

"No, you're not. You always said it was a heap of junk." The DI sounded tearful, so Carlos took the phone off speaker and turned away from the paramedics, lowering his voice. "But it was your heap of junk, Fiona. Your home. We need to talk."

Sara stepped back slightly to give him privacy and watched as the paramedics helped him to his feet after ruling out any serious injuries.

"I take it you have a key to this place?" the woman asked Carlos when he ended the call.

"In my coat pocket," he replied.

As they moved indoors, Sara reflected on the men she

had seen and the turmoil enveloping her beloved city. Gary gave his statement to a senior officer before saying goodnight to her. There was an odd look in his eyes that Sara couldn't interpret. Perhaps he was worried she might mention his drinking, but all she cared about was helping Carlos and Lady and fulfilling DI Cook's request. Gary had disappointed her this evening, and she knew a tough conversation awaited them; that was just another item to add to her growing to-do list.

13

Fiona plodded into Carlos's office, her shoulders sagging as she shook her head again and again. The paramedics were packing up their things, and one look from Fiona hurried them along. Fiona's wild hair was sticky with streaked ash from the fire, and her precious raincoat was more black than blue.

When she looked at Carlos, her eyes widened, unable to disguise the shock of seeing his face.

Carlos was lost for words as his friend slumped into a chair. Even Lady held back from her usual exuberance temporarily, but she herself was still clingy.

"It appears we've all been in the wars tonight," Carlos found his voice, forcing a smile. His lips wouldn't move in the way he wanted them to. The ice the paramedics had applied to his face had reduced some of the swelling, but he found it difficult to form facial expressions, let alone speak.

Sara had stayed with him the whole time. Lady had gone backwards and forwards between the two of them but mostly stayed with her head on Carlos's knee. With Fiona staying quiet, Lady walked over to her and licked her hand by way of welcome. Fiona leaned forward and stroked her.

"I see you've not quite recovered from your traumatic evening, Lady," she said. Fiona still had her smoky coat on, which made Carlos grimace. His eyes fixed on the arms of the chair where soot had left its mark. At least his ordered brain was still functioning. Sara had quietly made drinks and placed a mug of coffee in front of Fiona.

"Thanks." The drink had the effect of bringing Fiona out of a trance. She reached for the mug and spoke to Carlos. "Tonight wasn't what I was expecting for sure. The audacity of this man to think he can intimidate a detective inspector and a private investigator."

"If it hadn't been for Sara, Lady would be..." The words wouldn't come out.

Fiona's eyes softened from blazing anger to compassionate understanding. "I know, Carlos. But she's safe now."

Carlos looked at Fiona, feeling a tightness in his chest. "They even threatened Rachel."

"OMG. How on earth do they know about Rachel? That's an idle threat. They can't possibly get to anyone on board a cruise ship docked in New York."

"No, I don't believe they can. They obviously know where she is, but I don't think they'd be able to get to her."

"You should warn her all the same," Fiona's tone was serious.

"I will because the point is, they're scared, and it's made them unpredictable."

Fiona's eyes moved from Carlos to Sara, an uncertainty settling in the atmosphere.

"Would you like me to go, Ma'am?" Sara offered.

"If you wouldn't mind. I don't want to put you in danger, and Carlos and I need to talk."

Sara broke eye contact and gave a heavy sigh as she picked up her coat.

"I'll always be grateful to you, Sara, for..." He felt his voice cracking again.

"Yeah, we appreciate it, Sara," Fiona echoed. "I'll be in touch about what happened tonight. We'll need to take a statement."

"Gary and I gave our statements to the sergeant who attended, but of course, Ma'am. Whatever you say. Sorry about your home, Ma'am."

Fiona's eyes briefly misted over. "Yeah, me too."

After Sara left, Carlos said. "She's a good cop, Fiona. I think she was disappointed not to stay."

"I can't help that," Fiona waved a hand in the air before her eyes locked onto Carlos's. "We've got more important things to think about than a PC's hurt feelings. If tonight was a warning, I don't know what the next thing's going to be." She took a large gulp of coffee.

Carlos grimaced and stroked Lady. "Then we need to get them before they do any more damage."

"Are you sure you still want to be involved with this? It's turned out to be worse than either of us was prepared for. I have to carry on, but you don't."

"They were going to kill my dog, and they threatened my wife," Carlos answered, feeling a deep anger and determination. "Too right I need to carry on. This is now personal. We're obviously close to something we don't understand yet. We have to go back through everything. Somewhere in there is the key."

"It has a lot to do with this Mr Cross," said Fiona. "If we find him, or at least discover what happened to him, we might find who did this to you, or more importantly, who gave the order."

"They did it to you too," Carlos stared at her. "I'm not sure about what happened tonight. Maybe this has more to do with what Angel and Jodie Whitwick discovered. There's something big at play here. Bigger than normal for them to go to such desperate measures."

"Yeah, it's sloppy of Nicolae," Fiona said. "I don't remember him operating as blatantly as this. Threats, yes, even attacks, but not so openly. And his threats were more subtle. Taking us on when he knows how tenacious we are seems out of character."

"I've been wondering the same thing. Perhaps there's someone else. Another player we haven't yet identified."

"I'm open to suggestions," said Fiona. "What did Julie find?"

"To be honest, I didn't get time to look last night and had a few things to do at home before meeting you."

"You've had plenty of time since my home burnt down!"

Carlos gave her an astonished look. "Now I know you're joking. But..." He tried to laugh, but the pain in his ribs stopped him.

"Ouch," Fiona said, scrunching up her face.

"Yeah. Cracked rib. Paramedics don't think it's broken,

but it's still excruciating when I make any sudden movements."

"They really gave you a good working-over, didn't they?" said Fiona.

"It was nothing compared to the pain in my heart when they dragged Lady out of the car park, whining and struggling to get free. The thought of that being the last time I was ever going to see her was unbearable. If Sara and PC Gary Hodge hadn't been out for a meal, it could have ended very differently."

"So Hodge is in your good books."

"He arrived at the right time with Sara, but she's amazing, Fiona. Considering what she'd been through herself. She actually confronted these guys, not knowing if Gary would back her up. She told me Lady broke free when she distracted them and they made themselves scarce."

"And Gary Hodge?"

"Backed her up to the hilt. He was off duty but certainly went over and above his duty tonight."

"You look exhausted. Are you going to be able to sleep?" Fiona asked.

"I feel tired enough now the shock's wearing off. You look pretty deadbeat yourself. Why don't you take the bed upstairs and I'll sleep down here?" Carlos offered.

"Oh no," said Fiona. "You take the bed. You need it more than I do. I'll be fine down here. But before we do that, let's look at what Julie found out. Where's the file?"

"Move the chair you're sitting on and lift the rug."

Fiona did as she was asked and saw the loose board.

"We decided we'd keep important documents down

there after the previous break-in. They wouldn't have found anything vital if they had forced the filing cabinet. But they didn't come in here; they waited outside after smashing the security light in the car park."

"I see," said Fiona, retrieving the file and returning everything to its place. This time she removed her coat before flopping down in the chair again. "Shall I do the honours?"

"Go ahead," said Carlos.

"Why don't I get us both a glass of water?" Fiona suggested.

"You could do with washing your face while you're at it, if you don't mind me saying so."

"I had a go in the pub toilet, but the sink was the size of a dessert bowl." Fiona gave him a scathing look as she moved into the small cloakroom. He heard an exclamation. "Oh my word, I had no idea I looked that bad!" she said. "My neck is almost as bad as my hair."

"But not nearly as messy," Carlos called out, but suffered the consequences as his lip bled.

After cleaning herself up, Fiona went to the kitchen and returned with two glasses of water. She sat down and picked up the file again. "I forgot to tell you about the hippie neighbours."

Carlos tried to raise an eyebrow, but winced at the effort.

"In brief, a couple moved into a houseboat three down from mine a couple of months ago. They're a throwback from the flower-power era. Anyway, they told me my brother was on my boat, which rang alarm bells."

Carlos tried to sit forward, but Fiona waved a hand. "Steve's fine. I spoke to him after the fire, but I interviewed the couple afterwards in the local. Unfortunately, they spend most of their days stoned, so they weren't much help, but they said the guy was tall and stocky, nothing like Steve at all. Apart from that, they were useless and were disappointed at realising they were living so close to a detective."

Carlos wondered if they would be happy about Fiona's burnt houseboat but couldn't imagine anyone being that callous. "Did any of your neighbours see anything?"

"I left uniform to interview the ones who tried to help, and I'll get Hugh Barber to go boat-to-boat tomorrow." Fiona opened the file she was holding. "Okay, let's see what we've got here. First off, nothing that we didn't already know. Julie listed the nights of the unusual riots and everything she told us about the nights of the deaths. The jewellery theft and the council offices and councillor's home office break-in occurred after Angela and Diane had been killed but before Jodie. Tony Hadden has filled––"

"Stop a minute!" Carlos interrupted.

"What?" asked Fiona.

"I phoned Tony on my way back to the office to ask to meet for lunch tomorrow. He asked me to go round to his place then, but when I was almost there, he called it off, saying it could wait."

"Maybe you'd better phone him now," said Fiona.

"What time is it?"

"Late, but do it anyway."

Carlos grabbed his phone and dialled, but it went straight through to Tony's answerphone. "Voicemail. He might have gone to bed. It was weird because he sounded like he had something important to tell me before fobbing me off."

"Hold that thought." Fiona picked up her mobile and dialled. "It's DI Cook. Can you get someone to check on Mr Tony Hadden... What? Seriously?" Fiona pressed the speaker button so that Carlos could hear.

"Yes, Ma'am, we got a call from him. He thought burglars were attempting a break-in. He said his security cameras were down, but when we got there, there were no signs of a break-in."

"Did anyone go inside?"

"Yes, Ma'am, the door was unlocked. The PCs checked his security, and it was all working fine. There was an answerphone message with a lead in London. In his hurry, he must have left the door unlocked. The officers said footage from the security system showed his car leaving. The desk sergeant said the caller sounded like he'd been drinking, so maybe he made a mistake."

Fiona gritted her teeth. "If he'd been drinking, I'd like his car traced. Put someone on that, will you? I need to speak to him. I want a phone call the minute you find him."

"Yes, Ma'am, but he might not have been drinking."

Fiona shrugged irritably. "Just find the car. Check security cameras on the M1." She put the phone down.

Carlos sighed heavily. "If it weren't for his calling about the break-in, I'd say it was plausible. But if they don't find him by morning..."

"It sounds as though another story came up, Carlos, and he went out again. That ties in with what he told you."

"You might be right, but it's just that tonight of all

nights, with all that's been going on, I'm finding it hard to accept anything as being normal. Go on with what else is in the file."

Fiona buried her head in the file. "Tony Haddon had more or less told Julie what we'd found out about this person who groomed young women. It hadn't been a big enough story for him, so he hadn't followed it through. There was little evidence, and he had other priorities. Right... here's something interesting. This might be the other player we were talking about."

Carlos tried to lean forward in the chair again but grimaced as a sharp pain shot through his rib, making it difficult to breathe. His hand went to the pain, and Lady moved to his side immediately, putting her head on his knee. "I really must stop doing that," he said, taking a gulp of water. He laid a hand on Lady's head. "It's all right, girl. I'm okay. Everything's fine now." Lady didn't look convinced and stayed where she was.

"Jodie Whitwick wasn't only unpopular with the liberals for her extreme religious views and her anti-prostitution stance. She also butted heads with a wealthy property developer, persuading Planning to turn down his application. This was all going against the recommendations of a planning officer called Patricia Chen."

"Interesting."

Fiona met his gaze. "These are multi-million-pound planning applications. This guy, Michael Kingsland, has been snapping up vacant land. He's even put in applications to build on green belt land, with the same planning officer recommending they pass. It appears Jodie

Whitwick didn't like him, or his tactics, and had made sure his applications were repeatedly turned down. And guess what?"

"Go on." Carlos said.

"He has a major application up for a decision at Thursday night's planning meeting."

Carlos leaned back thoughtfully. "So her death could be all about planning and not about the sex trade or Nicolae. I'm wondering if we have a double-headed snake here."

Fiona continued reading. "Michael Kingsland has been investigated a few times after being accused of intimidation tactics. Threatening homeowners who won't sell up and that sort of thing. He's always lobbying councillors, and according to Tony Hadden, bribes might be involved. All without evidence. The only person Kingsland carried no sway with was Jodie Whitwick, who, Tony told Julie, was incorruptible."

"It's a leap from intimidation to murder, but clearly this developer has a lot to gain from her death. Where does that fit with the sex workers?"

"It's another leap to imagine him being involved in that, but not so difficult to imagine that he might have had some involvement in what we experienced tonight. If Jodie had something we could use against him, maybe he's scared we'll find it."

"So he could have been involved in Jodie's death and tried to make it look like it was linked to the sex worker murders, diverting police attention to the sex trade. But now he's frightened about our investigation. How would he know about us?" Carlos asked.

"Through a mole in Tony Hadden's office. I bet he got wind of Tony's conversation with Julie."

Carlos leaned back in his chair again. "That makes much more sense than Nicolae being so reckless and doing something as stupid as what happened to us."

"I agree," said Fiona. "So tomorrow, I realise it's Sunday, but you should track down your mate Tony and have a chat with Jodie's husband. I'll follow through on interviews with the boating community, and you should get some rest."

"What about Michael Kingsland?"

"I'll need to update the Super first thing Monday morning. We'll talk to him after that."

Carlos moved painfully in the chair. "Okay, Fiona. On that note, it really is time for me to try to get some sleep. Are you sure you don't want upstairs because I can't see me making it?"

"You need a decent night's sleep, mate," she said. "Come on, me and Lady will help you up."

"If you insist." Carlos struggled to his feet.

Fiona opened the secret door that led to the upstairs flat, and Lady bounded up ahead of them. "So much for her helping," Fiona groaned.

"Don't make me laugh, Fiona. It hurts."

14

As the reality of losing her precious houseboat hit, the floodgates opened. Fiona's tears came in waves. First, there was the anger, hot and fierce, and then came the grief. After tossing and turning, she sat up, hoping Carlos was having a better night after his painkillers. She wiped her face and stood up. There was a job to be done. People were dead, and Princess or some other poor soul might be next if she didn't pull herself together.

She splashed warm water on her face in Carlos's tiny cloakroom, looking at her reflection in the mirror. The woman staring back at her had red-rimmed eyes and smoke-streaked clothes. She hadn't bothered undressing, and the blanket Carlos had loaned her was now filthy. No doubt it would go straight into the washing machine when he found it. Fiona's hair, always wavy and wild, was worse than usual. She reeked of burnt timber and petrol. What she didn't enjoy was the fact that she looked ten years older. How could one age so much in one night? Fiona gripped the edge of the sink, her knuckles white, and forced herself to breathe. In through the nose, out through the mouth. The breathing exercises helped.

When she felt steady enough, Fiona telephoned the night sergeant. “It’s DI Cook. Did you get anywhere with finding Hadden?”

“Sorry, Ma’am.”

“Is there no sign of the car?”

Fiona heard a heavy sigh from the other end of the phone and prepared herself for what he was going to say. “To be honest, we’re stretched tonight, Ma’am. We’ve still got officers at the marina and those who attended Mr Jacobi have just finished filing their report. They should have gone home hours ago. There are two reported burglaries, a domestic violence incident, drug driving and—”

At least they have a home to go to, she thought before snapping. “Okay, I get it. You’re too busy to chase CCTV when we don’t know if a crime’s been committed.” Fiona ended the call, annoyed. The mention of the marina hadn’t helped her mood. Her home. Her sanctuary. Gone. Just like that.

At least Lady was safe upstairs with Carlos, but Tony Hadden might not be. The thought gnawed at her. Who could she call at this time of night? She checked her watch, nearly 3 a.m. Most people would be in bed.

Paul. The name popped unbidden into her head. No, she couldn’t. Wouldn’t. Resisting the urge to drag the man from his slumber, Fiona glanced at the stairs leading to where Carlos lay injured. The people who had hurt Carlos, stolen Lady and burned her home to ash wanted her frightened and useless. She wouldn't give them the satisfaction.

Fiona scribbled a note to Carlos and left by the rear entrance, taking his spare keys and ensuring the door was locked behind her.

After driving along country lanes for around forty-five minutes, heading nowhere in particular, the tears started again, affecting her vision. Fiona pulled into a lay-by. The car bounced as it hit a pothole. She switched the engine off and gripped the steering wheel so hard, her fingers ached.

Then the dam broke. Again.

She sobbed. Deep, wrenching sobs that came from somewhere primal. She cried for the loss of her home, for all the memories that had burned with it. The photos of her mum, who had died years before, of her dad, and the one of her and her brother as children. These were the things that were irreplaceable.

She cried because criminals still knew how to use her brother to get to her.

But most of all she cried for the loss of her father. The realisation hit her with the force of a physical blow. In all the heartbreak, Fiona realised she hadn't cried when her dad died. She'd stayed strong, arranged everything, and when it came to the funeral, there were his old friends and his caregivers to comfort. Packing his things into boxes, taking most of them to a charity shop had been so hard, but not as hard as feeling so alone.

As soon as she got back to work, she'd been handed a triple homicide and a bungled investigation into the first deaths. She had worked fourteen-hour days and survived on junk food and coffee, telling herself that work would heal her.

She hadn't healed, and she'd barely coped.

All the tears she'd bottled up were now spilling over, leaving her gasping for air. Her chest heaved. Her throat burned. She had witnessed overwhelming grief when informing relatives of the death of loved ones. She prided herself on empathy, but now she realised she hadn't had a clue.

Fiona got out of the car, stumbling slightly as her legs threatened to give way. She paced the lay-by, her breath coming in short, sharp gasps. Then she screamed at the top of her voice, releasing all the rage, pain, and frustration she'd been holding in. Paul had tried to counsel her, but she wouldn't have it.

Anyone hearing her now would think she needed locking up. The thought made her laugh, a wild, slightly hysterical laugh.

Just to fit her mood, the rain started, gentle at first with soft drops and then a torrent. Within seconds she was drenched, her smoke-stained coat clinging to her body, her hair dripping water. She pulled the raincoat over her head and ran back to the car.

Once inside, it was as if a switch had been flicked off. The tears stopped. The sky was doing all the crying for her, and it was doing a much better job. Rain drummed on the roof. Paul would say God was crying with her. The thought made her smile.

She blew her nose on a soggy tissue from her pocket and wiped her eyes with the towel she kept for the windows. She sat, exhausted but lighter somehow. The crying had released a pressure valve, and she no longer felt like she was going to explode.

Fiona turned the ignition, listening to the engine's familiar rattle. She patted the steering wheel. "At least they didn't get to you," she said before putting the car into gear. The headlights cut through the rain-darkened countryside as she turned around and headed for an all-night café.

The food after her meltdown would comfort Fiona more than any human being could have done. What did that say about her? But she loved food and paid the price with the extra weight. Not that she cared about that. Her weight might be an issue to others, but it had never been an issue to her. Life was too short to spend it counting calories or worrying about what dress size she wore.

The café on the outskirts of the city was open twenty-four hours a day. A handful of customers were scattered around. A couple of lorry drivers, an exhausted-looking nurse still in uniform, and a young couple with a screaming baby.

She ordered the all-day breakfast with eggs, bacon, sausage, beans, mushrooms, tomatoes and black pudding, served with two slices of toast. When it arrived, she tucked in with enthusiasm. For the first time in hours her mind switched off. All that existed was the food, the strong hot tea, and the normality of eating.

Now that she was all cried out and her stomach was full,

she turned her thoughts back to the murder investigation. She wiped her hands on a paper napkin and pulled out her phone. Prior to the boat-burning episode, Fiona had made notes. She scrolled through them.

The name Mr Cross stared at her from the screen with a large question mark next to it.

"Who are you, Mr Cross?" she muttered aloud. "And more importantly, where are you?"

The pieces were all there, scattered across crime scenes, multiple interviews, and multiple lives somehow entwined. She just needed to fit them together. All she knew for certain was that Nicolae was involved. The man was like a spider sitting in the centre of a vast web, controlling, numbing and ready to pounce.

The thought made her give an involuntary shiver. If Nicolae had Jodie Whitwick killed, had he done it as a favour for Michael Kingsland? That would be his style: creating debts that could be called in later.

"Of course," Fiona palm-slapped her head, drawing a curious glance from the lorry driver at the next table. It made sense that two men like that would work together.

Nicolae and Michael Kingsland. The sex trafficker and the property developer. On the surface, they moved in completely different worlds. But scratch beneath, and they were the same breed. Ruthless men who saw people as obstacles to be removed or resources to be exploited. Men who believed the rules didn't apply to them.

Kingsland wanted planning permission. Jodie Whitwick stood in his way and was, no doubt, a thorn in Nicolae's side.

Nicolae had the resources to make interfering people disappear.

But why kill the sex workers? Unless they knew something. Saw something. Or maybe they were just collateral damage, killed to muddy the waters, to make the police think they were hunting a serial killer when really it was just good old-fashioned greed and they were convenient decoys.

Tony Hadden might know who Kingsland's associates were. Tony made it his business to know things, to collect secrets and information like other people collected stamps. But where was Tony?

They needed to find Tony. And she needed to dig into Michael Kingsland's background, find out exactly what he'd been up to, who he'd been meeting with, what planning applications he had pending.

Thursday night's planning meeting. That's what Julie's notes had said. Four days away. If they were right, if part of this was about planning permission, then Kingsland was getting desperate. The warnings proved it. He was running scared, making mistakes.

But scared men were dangerous men.

Fiona drained the last of her tea, left a generous tip on the table, as the young waitress looked like she needed it. Fiona headed outside. The rain had eased to a drizzle. The worst of the storm had passed. She stood by her car for a moment, breathing in the clean, wet air, washing away the last lingering smell of smoke.

Time to catch a killer. But first, she needed clothes!

15

After a fitful night's sleep and two doses of codeine and anti-inflammatory tablets, Carlos woke with Lady nudging his arm. Whilst he ached from head to toe, the medication and rest had done a half-decent job. Forcing his eyes open, he checked the time. "No wonder you're complaining," he said to Lady as he blinked to recheck what he was seeing. 2 p.m., Carlos never slept in. He would need to make sure he didn't overdo the codeine tablets.

Sitting up slowly, he tested his pain levels. The worst was on his right side over the ribcage, but his face didn't feel as swollen, perhaps a combination of the icepacks and the anti-inflammatories the paramedics left him with. He swung his legs over the side of the bed and checked his phone. A voicemail from Tony Hadden half-reassured him that his friend was okay.

'Sorry I can't make lunch, Carlos. Something came up. Call you soon.'

At least it was contact, and as for lunch, Carlos would have missed it, anyway.

Lady moved around happily, wagging her tail, but was careful not to paw at him. She never failed to amaze him with her sixth sense.

"I'm sorry, girl, breakfast will have to wait. It might take me a while to get washed and dressed. First, I need to call for a windscreen replacement."

As if understanding, Lady returned to the bed he kept in the apartment for her. Thankful she had a good bladder; he made the telephone call. The brilliant thing about windscreen cover was the speed at which the company would come out to replace it. It would be repaired by the time he was up and dressed. Carlos slowly did what he needed to do.

When he eventually made it downstairs and let Lady out, he wasn't surprised to find Fiona gone. The note said simply: gone for a drive.

Not one to share her emotions, Fiona would need time to process her losses. She'd suffered her fair share of trauma in a short space of time. First, the death of her father, and now losing her home along with everything she owned apart from a Mini that was almost too old to be on the road and certainly too small for her. Carlos hoped any insurance policy she held would give her enough money to put a deposit down on a bricks and mortar home. He questioned whether that was the right way for Fiona. She loved her old boat, the freedom it provided, and the boating community who minded their own business. A house with foundations, a mortgage, and aloof neighbours would be wrong for someone like her. Not that she chatted to her neighbours at the marina, but they were a small community who looked out for each other when necessary.

When he woke in the middle of the night, he remembered Lady on his bed for the first time, but maybe he imagined it. She never slept on the bed. He'd trained her to sleep in her own bed, establishing that boundary. He didn't mind her abandoning the rule for one night, but it couldn't become a habit. She continued following him around as if attached to his legs. Walking was hard enough without the danger of being tripping over an overanxious dog who insisted on staying within inches of him. She shadowed his every step. When he stopped, she pressed against his legs.

Carlos made it to the kitchen and managed to make a mug of tea, but struggled to fill his dog's bowls with food and water. It was an effort to put them on the floor, but he managed it. At least it meant he could move cautiously back to the front office without landing on the floor. He laid the mug down and eased himself into the chair, trying not to jar his ribs.

Lady wolfed down her food and arrived back at his side. He leaned forward and stroked her ears, running his fingers through the silky fur. She sighed in contentment.

"Look, girl. We've both had some trouble," he mumbled. She watched him, her head cocked to one side, listening. "But this isn't going to work. If you want me to stay in one piece, you need to back off a bit, okay?"

Lady whined as if understanding but not wanting to obey. Her tail gave a half-hearted wag, but she stayed close.

Carlos sipped his tea and let his thoughts return to the night before and to the investigation. He was almost certain now that Nicolae hadn't been responsible for last night. It wasn't his style. If Nicolae wanted them out of the way, they would have disappeared for good. He wouldn't draw that kind of attention to his operation unless he planned to pack it in and move elsewhere. These attacks were an arrogant attempt to intimidate with hardly any thought to the consequences. Whoever ordered them was sloppy. The message, loud and obvious, came with all the finesse of a sledgehammer.

Carlos opened his tablet and began reading everything he could find about Michael Kingsland. The developer's career was a masterclass in aggressive business practices. He built his empire by buying up cheap land and developing it. What happened last night was the type of intimidation that appeared to be in Kingsland's wheelhouse. Every article written about Kingsland revealed him as an impatient man who always got his own way. The man wanted what he wanted, when he wanted it, and didn't take no for an answer. He was prone to temper tantrums and notorious for hiring and firing staff on a whim. He also threw a considerable amount of money into local politics, giving him the influence he craved.

The developer was now on his and Fiona's radar, so it would come as no surprise to discover the goons who attacked Carlos and burnt Fiona's home were hired by Kingsland. Fiona thought there might be a mole working for the local newspaper, so that might be the source of Kingsland's knowledge. Tony could be in trouble. More than Carlos initially imagined. He reached for his mobile phone, wincing as the movement pulled his ribs. Lady's head shot up, alert to his discomfort. He gave her a reassuring pat and dialled Tony's number. It was answered after two rings.

"Hello, Carlos. Sorry about lunch. Things got hectic."

Carlos heaved an enormous sigh of relief. "I'm just pleased you're all right."

"Why wouldn't I be?" Tony's voice sounded unusually strained.

"Well, you called the police last night about a possible break-in, which turned out to be nothing." Silence stretched at the other end of the phone. Carlos could hear Tony breathing.

"Did I? Oh, yes. A little too much brandy, I'm afraid, and something went wrong with my security cameras. I got all neurotic about it. That all stems back to the accident."

"I understand." Carlos did understand a little of PTSD, having suffered from it himself for years. "But you were out when they got there."

"You're right. That's why I cancelled lunch; I had to go out. It's a story I'm working on."

"Weren't you over the drink-drive limit?"

"Erm… I don't think so."

Carlos didn't want to push him away. "Is your story related to the riots or the homicides?"

"No. Definitely not."

The answer came too fast. Tony was lying. This was the Tony that Carlos had visited in the hospital after his burns ordeal. When one of Nicolae's men had paid him a visit. Carlos recognised fear in his voice, certain the same thing had happened last night. If so, there was nothing he could do about it. Carlos didn't have any authority to offer Tony

Hadden protection from Nicolae. He could barely protect himself and Fiona. He and Fiona would have to deal with Nicolae without Tony's help.

"Well, it's good to hear your voice anyway," said Carlos, keeping his tone light.

"You're talking funny, Carlos. Are you okay?" Tony asked.

"Swollen lip. I had a run-in with some goons. There are certain people who don't want us to continue with our investigation."

"I'm sorry to hear that, Carlos. Is Fiona okay?"

"If you call having her houseboat burned down okay, she's fine. I expect you'll hear about it soon enough. It'll make a good story."

"To be honest, Carlos, I'm thinking about taking a step back. The pressure's catching up with me," Tony's voice had changed to wistful. "I've sold several big stories lately and made a lot of money. It's time to buy a house in Spain and leave the horrible British weather behind. I think the climate will suit my gammy old body better."

Now Carlos knew they'd got to him. Really got to him. Tony Hadden loved his work, and he loved Leicester.

"That's not so easy these days. Tony. Look, if anyone's threatened you, it's for a reason. You know something. Why don't you tell me about it?"

Silence again. Carlos waited.

"I don't know anything that would help you right now," Tony's voice was melancholic. "Maybe when we're two old men sitting on the beach having a drink, things might be different. But for now, I've got nothing for you."

Carlos closed his eyes, accepting the inevitable. Tony would not tell him anything else. Maybe it was better that way; at least he'd stay alive.

"Okay, Tony. I get it. You've suffered enough for your job."

"Thanks, pal. It's been good knowing you."

The finality in Tony's words made Carlos's throat tighten. "You're not leaving right away, are you?"

"I'm already here. My cousin's collecting me from the airport. I'll stay with her and her family for a while."

Carlos sensed Tony was being deliberately vague about exactly where he was and didn't want to press him on it. "What about your house and the story?"

"I can write the story from here. And restrictions mean I can only stay in Europe for three months initially, but I can apply for a longer visa, so we'll see. I'll come back and put the house on the market if I decide to apply for citizenship."

"Okay, Tony. We'll be following up on some leads you gave Julie. I'm sorry if I got you into a mess again. You deserve a good life."

"Kind of you to say so," Tony said quietly.

They said their goodbyes, which sounded awkward and insufficient for a friendship that had spanned years. Carlos ended the call and sat holding the phone, staring at Tony's name. Now what?

16

Following his call with Tony and tracking down Andrew Whitwick only to find a grief-stricken man staying in the Lake District with his parents and the children, Carlos felt like throwing the phone against the wall, when he heard the key turn in the lock. He initially tensed and his hand went to his ribs, but then he heard Fiona's voice.

"It's only me."

He relaxed as she appeared in the doorway. She looked better than she had when he'd gone to bed. Her hair was clean, and she seemed to be wearing new clothes. She hung her now clean, but ancient raincoat on a peg and joined him, handing him a takeaway beefburger and chips in a cardboard box.

"What about you?" he asked, accepting the offering.

"I had a greasy meal in a diner this morning and lunch at a carvery. Then I popped into the office to catch up with Hugh and the stroppy DC, Caroline Maplin. Both gave up their day off today to interview people down at the marina.

By the way, there's a guy in a van outside changing your windscreen. He's almost finished." She flopped into the chair opposite him.

"That's brilliant. I'll go and see him."

Once Carlos signed the paperwork for the new windscreen, he went back to his armchair to tackle his burger. "Any leads?" he asked.

Fiona shook her head. "A jumbled mass of sightings, but most of them will be walkers or people feeding the swans further down. They often stray into the marina and look at the moorings." Fiona pointed to his food. "I know it's not your usual diet, but you need to eat something, and despite the name, I'm no cook."

"Nevertheless, I appreciate it. I'm not long up and haven't eaten so anything to soak up the medication from last night will help." He took a bite, and despite his preference for healthy food, the fatty comfort food was satisfying. He was hungrier than he had realised.

Fiona's swollen eyes gave away the emotional toll from the pain of losing her home, and he didn't blame her. He understood. He'd wept like a baby when the men took Lady. Sometimes you had to cry because holding it in was worse than letting it out, even if his outburst had made his attackers feel more powerful.

"Did you get time to find Tony Hadden?"

"He's in Spain, would you believe?"

Fiona raised an eyebrow. "Something happened at his place last night, then?"

"Not that he'll admit, but I'm sure of it. He's talking retirement."

"To be honest, I don't want his death on my conscience, so perhaps he's making the right choice."

"I also contacted Andrew Whitwick," Carlos said.

"And from the look on your face, that didn't help either."

Carlos swallowed the food in his mouth before answering. "He's a broken man, Fiona. He couldn't tell me anything about Jodie's work because they put a protective ring around their family time. When they worked, they worked, and when they were together, their relationship with their children took priority. That and the church."

Fiona's eyes seemed far away. "I wish I'd been able to do that. I hardly ever visited my dad."

Carlos felt a pang reminding him of how much he missed Rachel. He didn't know what he'd do without her. "Your father knew how much you loved him, and I don't feel distant from Rachel even though she's in New York. We love each other, and that's what matters. Perhaps if we have children, things will change. Anyway. Andrew is on compassionate leave and staying with his parents in the Lake District indefinitely."

"Another dead end." Fiona's lips formed into an amused smile. "On the plus side, your face looks better already."

Carlos raised an eyebrow. "You're a terrible liar, you know that?"

"One of my few failings." She studied him for a moment as if cataloguing his injuries in the daylight.

"I take it you found time to go clothes shopping?" He didn't mention that Fiona no longer smelled of burnt charcoal.

"I found an Asda and bought as many cheap dresses as possible that would fit, along with other items that you don't need to know about."

He grinned despite the pain it caused his lip. "I'm married, remember. I do know that women like to change their underwear."

"Then I showered at the station and stopped by a launderette to get my old clothes washed and dried."

"You have been busy." Carlos took another bite of his burger, chewing slowly. His jaw ached from where a goon had punched him. "You didn't think to buy a new raincoat?"

"Some things you need to hang onto, Carlos, especially when you've already lost so much." Her voice threatened to break, but she held it together, her hands gripping the arms of the chair. "Did you phone Rachel?"

"Not yet. I don't want her to see my face like this just yet. I can't help feeling I shouldn't have involved Tony again." The guilt added to his physical pain.

"Look, Carlos." Fiona leaned forward, her elbows on her knees. "Tony wanted the story, and you gave it to him. To keep writing about crime in this city, he was bound to cross Nicolae again now that the guy's back. It was just a matter of time."

Perhaps she was right, and Tony's fate had been sealed the moment Nicolae returned to Leicester. It didn't make Carlos feel any better about it. "I've been reading up on Michael Kingsland. He's a real piece of work."

"Yeah, I did the same. Hopefully, we'll speak to him tomorrow. The super called me to say she heard about the boat and wants an update first thing. Are you okay with me sleeping on the sofa for another night?"

"Sure, but take this as a temporary solution." Carlos opened his wallet and handed her a key. "That's the house in Oadby. Stay as long as you like. I'll be crashing in the flat for a while."

Fiona's eyes misted over as she took the key. "Thank you. I'll try not to stay too long; I've got to call the insurance company. I can't remember if the policy covers temporary accommodation."

"Use the landline. I'm going to take Lady for a walk."

"Are you sure?"

"Castle Gardens is not too far, and we both need the air. I'll pop some pills before I go. Help yourself to anything."

"You're a good friend, Carlos. I'll make the calls and go to your place in Oadby. At least that way, you'll get some rest."

"See you tomorrow, then."

"You can count on it."

Carlos opted for anti-inflammatories and paracetamol because he wanted to keep his faculties. The paramedics had told him to keep moving but not to do anything too strenuous. A quick stroll would have to do, and he needed to make sure his neurotic dog tasted normality because he couldn't risk her getting PTSD as well. He didn't put the lead on Lady, not wanting to risk being pulled, but commanded her to keep to heel as they left.

17

Sara Ransom stared absentmindedly through Suki's flat window overlooking the clock tower where all her troubles started. Boredom threatened to overwhelm her as she pondered whether to visit Carlos Jacobi. Not sure of the protocol between professional and friendly concern, she decided against it. DI Cook might not see a visit from Sara as genuine concern. Being honest with herself, Sara wanted to see Lady, the dog she'd rescued, as much as she did Carlos. It was a miracle that she and Gary had been out for dinner so close to the crime, and she shuddered to think what would have happened to Lady if they hadn't left when they did.

Her eyes settled on the clock tower again, her mind reliving the trauma of finding Jodie Whitwick's body. Sara watched a huge Black man cross the square and stop to talk to a couple of burly white guys. Memories tried to surface as Sara studied the black guy. Maybe she recognised him from school, but when he looked up, it clicked. *That's the man who attacked me*. She reached for her phone and zoomed in on his eyes. They were the eyes of the man who had thrust a broken bottle into her head, and also, she remembered why he seemed familiar. He lived on the same street as a cousin, near to where Sara and her mum lived.

"Gotcha."

Sara grabbed her coat and hurried downstairs, unsure what to do next. Without evidence, her recollection would be dismissed. After all, how could she be one hundred percent certain it was him? And yet... She hid in a doorway, watching the men while pretending to window-shop. The man – Tyson Jerome, she remembered his name – didn't look her way. Whatever he and the other men were talking about, the conversation was heated. Neither of them looked happy as Tyson gesticulated, giving the impression that he was telling them off.

After a while, the two men stormed off. Tyson looked around, and Sara quickly pulled her hood up just in time, turning to face the shop. She observed him through the window's reflection and saw him turn and swagger towards the market. The walk she also recognised as his. Sara wanted to run after him, put a hand on his shoulder and say, "You're nicked." But that's how it worked on television, not in real life, and her being off duty made it even more ridiculous. Initially, the break helped her heal, but now she itched to get back to work or leave. One or the other. Her head still ached as the stitches pulled.

In a split second, Sara decided to follow Tyson.

You never know, he might lead me to whoever organised

the unrest or who orchestrated the murders. She was pretty sure that's what had happened the night of her attack. Even though nobody had said it, she'd read the article in the local paper about the dead councillor whose body she'd discovered, grateful the reporter hadn't mentioned her name. It mentioned an off-duty police officer finding the body next to the tower, along with a religious pamphlet similar to the other two murders.

Rumours about a serial killer on the loose in Leicester made women in the city nervous. The article had continued with a large spread about the life and work of Jodie Whitwick. It described her as a vehement anti-prostitution campaigner, not afraid to speak out against what she said were women being enslaved and used. Many people interviewed described her as a bigot. Some believed she was right. To Sara, Jodie Whitwick was like a voice crying in the wilderness. In her opinion, men in power abused most sex workers.

Keeping her eye on Tyson, she watched him take a right turn, strolling the length of the streets behind the city's market. The smell of cabbage reached her nostrils as she walked. It was as if her nose tuned into the smell whenever she passed the market. Despite the multitude of fruit and vegetable stalls, the cabbage odour always assaulted her. Her dislike of the vegetable must make it that way.

Tyson bent down to tie his shoelaces. Sara ducked into one of the many shopping arcades running between the street they were on and the market. She felt breathless for a moment, wondering if he'd spotted her, but when he stood up, he set off at a faster pace as if in a hurry to get somewhere. She tried to keep pace with him while maintaining a safe distance. He walked the length of the road and turned onto the square where the Holiday Inn faced them and the Radio Leicester building on the left. He took the left turn, passing the cathedral and continuing his march. Sara followed. It looked as if he was heading towards the university. The streets were busy with traffic but quieter in terms of pedestrians, so she had to be careful. She lengthened the distance between herself and her quarry, pulling her hood tight around her head.

Tyson passed the university without glancing at it. Sara had spent three years of her life studying there. While reminiscing, she almost missed seeing Tyson enter a corner shop but turned her head just in time. She risked approaching the shop but didn't dare go inside. She stopped outside, pretending to look at something in the window while peering through the window displays. Her timing meant she saw Tyson hanging back while a woman paid the man behind the counter for her purchases. As soon as the woman left the shop, Tyson stepped toward the counter. Neither spoke as the man bent down and then handed Tyson a bundle of fifty-pound notes.

Sara's mind swirled, and her heart did a double somersault. What had she just witnessed, and what was she supposed to do about it? For all she knew, the payment could be legal, but she doubted it. Angry that it might be payment for the trouble of the night she was attacked, or that they were planning more in the future, it strengthened her resolve.

What if it was payment for the attack on Carlos, or the torching of DI Cook's boathouse? Although frightened, her rage at what they would have done to Lady gave her courage. She recalled the hatred in Tyson's eyes on the night he shoved the broken bottle into her head, and it made her even more determined to make sure he was arrested. Once more Sara ducked inside a doorway when he left the shop. She held her breath in case he came back her way. With her heart hammering in her chest, she realised she'd closed her eyes just like she did as a child, believing that no-one could see her if her eyes were shut. She opened them and poked her head around the doorway. Tyson's heavy frame had almost disappeared in the distance.

Now, what do I do? She debated whether she should enter the shop and ask questions or follow Tyson. The shopkeeper could wait. Sara quickened her pace to a brisk power walk verging on a jog. Tyson was walking faster, a man on a mission. It was almost as if the money in his jeans pocket was burning him; such was the urgency of his journey. They left the town centre behind them, Sara determined to see where he was going with the money. Why had the man handed over so much money in fifty-pound notes? It could be counterfeit or laundered money.

"Dumb idiot," she muttered, "you should have taken a photo."

Sara continued tailing Tyson for another fifteen minutes as he twisted and turned, almost as if aware of her presence. Was he just overcautious because of the money in his pocket, or had he spotted her? No, she reassured herself. If he had, he would have disappeared or challenged her. They continued the cat-and-mouse journey for another ten minutes until they reached the Foxdale estate.

At that moment, the rain came down. It was a good thing for Sara because she could pull her hood even tighter without looking odd. Everything but a small part of her face was covered. Nobody would recognise her.

Five minutes later, Tyson entered Foxdale Baptist Church.

What the heck is he doing here?

She skirted around the back of the building to stay hidden from the CCTV cameras and worked her way along the edge, keeping away from the car park. But she couldn't see or hear anything, so she moved cautiously, peering through each window. There was no sign of Tyson through the first two but then she glimpsed him. He was with a bigger man than himself, Pastor Paul Allen, whom she'd met a couple of times.

The two men walked into an office. Sara couldn't see much, nor hear anything, but this time she had her phone ready to take photos when Tyson exited. Minutes later she heard cars pulling into the car park, so she had to make herself scarce again. A group of six men got out of two cars, bypassed the main entrance and entered the church's annexe.

Sara snuck around front again, took photos of the cars, making sure the registration numbers were clear, and went back to the window in time to see Tyson shaking the pastor's hand. She snapped a photo without using flash and ducked down. Sara could hear the two men laughing and joking. Tyson headed towards the annexe where the men had gone. Stepping cautiously towards it, she saw a sign in the window listing dates and times of activities. Nothing was scheduled for this time.

She so wanted to go inside the building and ask the pastor about his business with this man, but she had no proof of anything and didn't want to give herself away if he was involved in something illegal.

Despite being convinced Tyson had attacked her, it would be impossible to prove it. If only she'd got hold of the broken bottle for DNA tests that night, but her first thought had been to protect herself, and then she'd been whisked away too quickly; Gary had seen to that. And by the time she arrived back at the clock tower and discovered the body on that fateful morning, the bottle was the last thing on her mind.

The only thing she had to go on now was the money exchange, and a suspicion that Tyson was up to no good. Without evidence of either, her time had been wasted.

"Hey! What are you doing?" A bulky guy with a limp bore down on her.

Startled for a moment, her teeth chattering and heart pounding lest the men inside came out, she remembered something on the list. "I... I'm er... checking the time of the next prayer meeting."

The man smirked, looking down at her, his eyes narrowed. "Did you get it?"

"Yes."

"Then you'd better be off."

Sara scuttled past him and heard him chuckling to himself as he pushed the doors open and entered the annexe. That was too close for comfort, she thought, hurrying away.

Deflated and frightened, Sara retraced her steps. She would tell Carlos Jacobi what she'd seen. Maybe he could make sense of it. She began the long journey back towards the city centre, hoping Carlos would be in his office. At least now she had a reason to visit.

18

Fiona arrived at the police headquarters and took the lift to the fourth floor. The carpeted flooring was a far cry from Fiona's office on the ground floor and the hub she used close to the city centre. When she arrived in front of the bulletproof glass door, Superintendent Henley's PA, Clara Fielding, didn't look up from her computer. Fiona pressed the bell and Clara pretended to be busy before deigning to buzz her through. Clara was her usual condescending self.

"Yes?"

Through gritted teeth, Fiona went through the ritual. "DI Cook to see Superintendent Henley."

"Take a seat, and I'll let her know you're here."

Fiona just wanted to get on with things, but she had to play Clara's game, or she would be even more obstructive than usual. The PA considered herself above anyone not based on the senior floor, and she was given latitude because she had worked for the superintendent for a long time. Too much latitude in Fiona's opinion.

Clara repeated her pretence of finishing something else before picking up the phone. "DI Cook to see you, Ma'am."

When she put the phone down, she slowly looked up at Fiona.

"You know the way." She swatted her away with a flick of the wrist. The irritating woman acted in the same way every time Fiona had a meeting with her boss.

Fiona took deep breaths as she walked to the familiar office and knocked.

"Come in!"

Fiona could immediately tell from the superintendent's face that she had a lot on her mind. Superintendent Henley was a decent officer who had shown herself incorruptible in the past, but she was also under constant pressure. The lines beneath her eyes and the greyer hair were indicators, but as she stood to shake hands before walking back to her desk, she was stoical. Standing at around five-ten, she towered over Fiona. Henley managed several DCIs, who managed DIs. Their past shared experiences meant the superintendent took a personal interest in Fiona and her work. Most likely, the three deaths Fiona was investigating also explained her interest at present. The pressure since a vocal councillor had been murdered would be mounting.

To Fiona, the status of a victim shouldn't matter, but it still did. Even in this day and age, those in prominent positions were given a higher priority than those who weren't. For her part, Fiona put the same effort into every murder.

Every life mattered to her. In fact, Angela and Diane's deaths mattered more because of the botched investigation. Since meeting Diane's husband, it wasn't fair that despite a failed marriage; he had to live with the fact that his ex-wife had been a sex worker and murdered. He seemed a decent sort, working a good job, trying to earn an honest living. Not that any of that had been enough for his wife.

Fiona took the seat opposite Henley's desk and waited for her to speak.

"DCI Flatley is in another meeting, but I'll update him later."

It seemed odd because Malcolm had texted her the night before to say he'd see her this morning. "Okay, I understand you want an update on the investigation?"

"I do, Fiona, but first, I'd like to ask how you are?"

The superintendent had never asked how she was before, not even after her father died. "Would you like a cup of tea or coffee?"

Fiona didn't want either, but knowing that the officious Clara Fielding would be called upon to make it, she couldn't help herself. "I'd love a cup of coffee, please, Ma'am."

Henley picked up the phone. "Could you bring two coffees, please, Clara?" She looked at Fiona. "Milk and sugar?"

"Milk, no sugar, thanks." With a self-satisfied grin, Fiona took more delight than she should have when Clara entered a few minutes later carrying a tray set with cups of coffee on saucers, a jug of milk, a bowl of sugar and a plateful of biscuits. Clara placed the tray on the table, preparing Superintendent Henley's drink with precision before adding milk to the other. She glared at Fiona. Fiona was pretty sure that if the superintendent hadn't been there, the PA would have slammed Fiona's cup down and slopped milk everywhere.

"Thank you, Clara. That will be all."

Dismissed back to her desk, Clara left the room with the poise of someone trying not to show how demeaning she found it to bring the likes of Fiona a hot drink. Fiona noticed a twinkle in Henley's eyes, suggesting she wasn't oblivious to her PA's antics.

"So, Fiona. How are you?"

"We're making progress, Ma'am."

"I'm talking on a personal level. You've just returned from compassionate leave, and now you've been handed this crap show. I know prominent people could be involved again, and I'd like to know how you're coping."

"Everything's fine, Ma'am. I prefer to be at work. It keeps me busy. I'd only sit around all day moping, and I don't have anywhere to sit anymore."

The super's eyebrows arched as she tried to show compassion. "I was coming to that. Of course I've heard about the unfortunate torching of your erm… home."

It was home to me, thought Fiona petulantly, but held her tongue.

"Do you believe what happened is linked to your investigation, or can we put it down to an unfortunate coincidence?"

"Not the latter, Ma'am; I'm certain it's linked." She didn't mention how somebody had pretended to be her brother because she didn't want to be taken off the case if Henley whiffed personal involvement. "Just as the fire started, a man wearing a balaclava pinned my arms behind me and warned me not to continue investigating."

A frown crossed the superintendent's face. "How dare they? Who do these people think they are?"

"Jacobi and I must have rattled someone's cage," Fiona said, taking a drink of coffee.

"Please tell me your boat was insured?"

"Yes, Ma'am, I'm waiting to hear to what extent."

"Do you have anywhere to stay in the meantime?"

"Yes, Ma'am. A friend has offered me the use of their house. They're staying in a flat in the city centre at the moment."

"That's something at least. When you say you believe you've upset someone, does that mean you're close to finding the perpetrator or perpetrators of these murders?"

The superintendent was done with the fluff and apparent concern for Fiona's well-being, but she was used to it. "Did you hear that Carlos Jacobi was attacked on the same night?"

Henley nodded. "How bad was it?"

"Pretty bad, Ma'am. He suffered a cracked rib, extensive bruising and injuries to his face. Nothing that won't heal, and thankfully no fractures. He's a tough cookie."

"And you believe the same people responsible for your boat attacked him?"

"Yes, I do. He received the same warning I did. We were both hit where it hurt. They took his dog and we're sure they were going to kill her as a warning to him to stay away. They even threatened his wife, who is currently working on a cruise ship."

The superintendent's eyebrows rose even more than they had the first time. "I don't like the sound of this, Cook. I don't like the sound of this at all."

"Me neither, but thanks to PCs Sara Ransom and Gary Hodge, the dog was rescued and returned to Carlos. That's when they found him injured and bound. They called the paramedics. Officers on duty took Ransom and Hodge's statements as they were off duty."

The superintendent steepled her hands under her chin. "Was the warning specific? How are these events linked to your investigation?"

"We don't know for sure, but what we know is – you remember the Romanian, Nicolae, who left the country after DCI Masters was arrested?"

"How could I forget?"

"You may also know that the evidence we had against Nicolae Romanescu disappeared shortly after he did."

Another frown crossed the superintendent's face. "I was aware of that and was told it was an administrative error. The documents were shredded by mistake."

"I don't believe it was a mistake, Ma'am. I believe it was deliberate so that he could return without being arrested."

"Are you telling me this man is in Leicester?" Henley's tight lips and frown made her look decidedly cheesed off.

"We believe so, Ma'am. I haven't managed to confirm it yet, but have heard and seen enough to believe he's back and up to his old tricks. Sex trafficking, modern slavery, drugs; you name it, he's got a finger in it. The only thing we lack is evidence."

"Evidence, I assume you're going to come up with soon."

"Trying to, Ma'am. We think there could be a connection between the murders and Nicolae. We also believe he might be involved with a property developer named Michael Kingsland."

Henley placed her cup firmly in its saucer before sitting back in her chair. "Now, just a minute. I know Michael Kingsland. He's a friend of the chief constable and has donated a lot of money to police charities. He's influential in political circles, and that makes him unpopular in some quarters."

"But he's not above the law, Ma'am."

"Of course not. If you can find a shred of evidence to back up what you're implying, I'll back you to the hilt, but tread carefully. I don't want pillars of the community upset over a hunch, that's all I'm saying."

"I suspect he's behind the burning down of my home and the Jacobi attack."

"What you suspect and what you can prove are two different things. Don't make this personal, Fiona. Do you have any evidence to back up this theory?"

"Not yet, Ma'am."

"Then I suggest you leave Mr Kingsland alone and look into Nicolae Romanescu?"

"We will. We believe Nicolae is behind the murders and the Tony Hadden incident."

Superintendent Henley's eyes narrowed as she straightened her uniform in frustration. "What Tony Hadden incident?"

"He's left the country."

"Is this Hadden the journalist whose article I read recently?"

"Yes, Ma'am."

"He was quite effusive about the late Councillor Jodie Whitwick, whom I also knew personally. I didn't always agree with her perspective, but I admired what she was trying to do and her good intentions. Anyway, that's going off the subject. Tell me more about Tony Hadden."

"Carlos arranged to meet him for lunch yesterday – before he was attacked, obviously. On the same night Hadden called the police, saying his CCTV had gone black and that intruders were about to enter his property. When the uniformed officers got there, everything was working fine. They checked the house and the security footage and found nothing. The night desk sergeant said he sounded drunk. Hadden's car left before the police arrived, and I asked them to trace his car. They were too busy." It still irked Fiona that they hadn't been able to speak to Tony before he left the country. "He cancelled lunch with Carlos and later told him he was in Spain. We believe he received a similar warning to ours, but the lack of violence and the level of fear suggest it came from Nicolae, who works differently and has a wider reach. When he acts, it's often difficult to trace it back to him."

"I don't understand how you believe Michael Kingsland is in league with this Nicolae. And what makes you think that Tony Hadden didn't decide to take a last-minute holiday? He might be stressed if he's imagining intruders are breaking in when they are not."

Fiona wanted to slam her hand down on the table and say that she just knew, but that would definitely get her thrown off the case. "We can't be certain, Ma'am, but Jodie Whitwick had become a pain in Kingsland's side. Judging by what I've read about the man, and what Tony told Carlos's PA before he decided he couldn't talk anymore, Kingsland is the impatient type. Intimidation tactics have been mentioned before."

"Look, Fiona," Henley's tone suggested she was losing patience. "You of all people shouldn't believe everything you read online or in the newspapers. Men like Michael Kingsland are successful, and there are those who resent success."

Perhaps, but Jodie Whitwick wasn't easily intimidated, thought Fiona, saying. "Jodie Whitwick's home and work offices were ransacked."

"Are you suggesting that Michael asked Romanescu to get rid of Jodie?"

"Paid, more likely," said Fiona. "Or called in a favour. But if I'm right, he now owes Nicolae a favour, which cannot be good for this city."

"You were right before about corruption, Fiona, but don't let your imagination run away with you. I know you're angry about what happened to your boat and to Jacobi, but keep things in perspective. I would rather you went after your chief suspect, Nicolae, and left Michael Kingsland – a legitimate investor in this city – alone."

Not gonna happen, thought Fiona, but recognised the time to stop pushing. "We're following a lead that might lead to Nicolae, Ma'am."

"You'd better get on with it then. I would like results, not hunches. Do you understand?"

Fiona drained her cup, allowing Henley to calm down. "I do, Ma'am. If you've got another five minutes, can I ask one more question?"

Superintendent Henley glanced at her watch. "Be quick."

19

WHEN FIONA ENTERED CARLOS'S OFFICE BUILDING via the back door, she heard voices and assumed Julie was in.

"I hope the kettle's on," she called.

"Only if you're putting it on," Carlos called back. Fiona filled the kettle and switched it on before making her way into his office.

It wasn't Julie he was speaking to; it was PC Sara Ransom who got up to make the drinks while Carlos sat in an armchair. Lady welcomed Fiona enthusiastically, seeming more like her usual self. Her tail wagged vigorously as Fiona leaned down to stroke her. Lady circled her with appreciative whines, although the canine kept Carlos in sight the whole time.

"Okay, Lady, that's enough," she said, taking another armchair. "No Julie?"

"It's her mum's birthday, so she had a day off planned. I didn't want her to cancel it, even though she offered."

"I take it she hasn't seen your rearranged face yet?" Fiona

chuckled at her own joke before adding, "which looks a lot better than it did on Saturday night."

"Ice and rest work wonders. You're just in time to hear what Sara's got to say."

Fiona exhaled. The last thing she wanted right now was to hear the PC's report. After her meeting with Henley, she just wanted to get out there and move the investigation forward. "We've got Sara's statement, Carlos."

"This is about something else. Sara saw the man who attacked her."

Fiona stood up again and removed her coat, throwing it over the back of a chair. She noticed a wince from Carlos, who liked meticulous order, but she wasn't in the mood. "In that case, tell me what you've got." Fiona eyed Ransom, who set coffee mugs down on the table and sat on a stool, seeming less enthusiastic about speaking to Fiona than she had to Carlos a few moments before.

"One thing I clearly remembered about my attack was the eyes of the man who shoved a broken glass into my head." Sara's hand moved subconsciously to her hairline where the stitches seemed to be healing well. "Hatred glared at me that night, and I wondered why. I thought I recognised the eyes but couldn't bring his identity to mind."

"But now you do?" Fiona wanted to hurry the story along.

"You may not know, Ma'am, but I'm staying in a friend's flat which overlooks the clock tower."

"No, I didn't know. Is it relevant?"

"There's no reason you should, but yes, it is." Sara continued, "I was looking through the window this morning when I thought I saw the man again. Then I realised it was him."

"How can you be certain when you said he was wearing a balaclava?"

"I zoomed in on his eyes with my phone camera. It was definitely him, and I know now why I thought I recognised him last week. He lives around the corner from my mum's. I usually live there, but I'm staying at my friend's until the stitches are out. My mum worries."

Fiona didn't have the time or the patience to go off-piste. "Recognising a man's eyes isn't enough to bring him in but give me his name and we'll check the PNC and H.O.L.M.E.S to see if he shows up." The PNC was the Police National Computer, which was due to be replaced in the next year, and H.O.L.M.E.S was the Home Office Large Major Enquiry System, an IT system primarily used for managing serious and complex crime investigations.

"Hear her out, Fiona," Carlos said. "There's more."

Fiona held up her palms in surrender, feeling glum. "Okay, I'm all ears."

"I followed him and—"

"You did what? Knowing how dangerous this man can be, you followed him while on sick leave without backup. That's the foolhardiest thing I've heard today."

Ransom looked mortified at the rebuke. Carlos intervened on her behalf again. "Please, Fiona, calm down and listen to what she's got to say."

"Sorry," she said. "It's not been a good morning so far, and being homeless doesn't make me the happiest bunny in the world. Now I'm hearing that an off-duty officer has been taking unnecessary risks and following a violent criminal." She shook her head, but took a drink of coffee.

"You're not exactly homeless," said Carlos. "You have keys to my house."

"Not the same," said Fiona, sulking. "All right, Sara, carry on. I apologise for interrupting. I still think it was foolhardy, but as you're in one piece, we'll leave it at that."

Sara's eyes shifted to Carlos, who gave her a nod of support. Even Lady crossed the room to place her head on Sara's knee protectively.

"Don't gang up on me," said Fiona with a smile, "just tell me what you found."

"He left town and passed the university until, a short while after, he stopped at a corner shop. I watched him go inside and then observed the shopkeeper handing Tyson – Tyson Jerome's his name – a rolled bundle of fifty-pound notes."

Fiona felt her jaw drop. "Now I'm interested."

"After he left the shop, I debated whether to go inside and speak to the shopkeeper or to keep following my attacker. I followed Tyson. His route was unusual, zigzagging all over the place as if he knew he was being tailed and wanted to shake someone off."

"Did he see you?"

"No, he turned to look behind every so often, but I kept a healthy distance and anticipated him, hiding every time he turned. I'm certain he didn't know I was following him because there were numerous streets where he could have disappeared and he would have lost me. It seemed more precautionary."

"So where did he go? Please tell me he met Nicolae, handed him the money, and you have a photo."

"I don't know who Nicolae is, Ma'am. He walked to the Foxdale estate, and I stayed with him." Sara hesitated, glancing at Carlos, who gave her a reassuring nod.

"Tell her."

"He went to Foxdale Baptist Church, Ma'am."

Fiona saw the sympathetic look Carlos gave her as she felt her heart drop into her stomach. Feeling breathless, she asked, tight-lipped. "What happened next?"

"I went round the back to avoid being seen. Then I made my way to the front and started looking through the windows. Eventually, I saw Tyson enter the pastor's office."

Fiona's heart burst against her chest as she fought an overwhelming desire to scream. She wasn't sure how much more bad news she could absorb. Lady sensed her distress and moved over to her. Fiona swore that dog had a sixth sense. "Anything else?"

"Five men arrived in two cars, so I had to hide around the corner again. I watched them go into the annexe."

"Did you recognise any of these men?"

"No, Ma'am. I couldn't risk being seen, but I took photos of the cars and the registration numbers before making my way back to the window. I was just in time to see Tyson leaving the pastor's office. They seemed friendly, laughing and joking."

Fiona didn't know which was the stronger emotion she was feeling now: rage or sorrow. A man she trusted, had feelings for, might be involved in this Nicolae racket. "What next?" she snapped.

"Tyson went into the annexe to join the men who arrived, and the pastor went back to his office."

"Did you hear anything?"

"No, I had to leave in a hurry because another man appeared out of nowhere and asked what I was doing. I talked my way out of trouble, but with it being such a close call, I decided to get away. I've got a couple of photos of the pastor with Tyson, that's all."

Fiona really didn't think things could get any worse. She'd been taken for a fool. Was Paul Allen on Nicolae's payroll? Just another of his slimy employees? She couldn't speak but tried to absorb the information. Confused thoughts and emotions made her feel lightheaded.

Carlos broke the silence. "Good job, Sara. You did well, but please don't put yourself at risk like that again. These people are dangerous."

"I agree with Carlos," Fiona forced herself to say something. "You did well. When are you due back at work?"

"On Thursday, Ma'am."

Fiona pushed down her emotions, deciding now was as good a time as any other, so she came out with what she had discussed with Superintendent Henley. "Would you like to be seconded to my team and consider an application to CID?"

Sara's eyes widened. "Me?"

"You've shown yourself tough in a crisis, a tad reckless maybe, but we can work on that. You showed following your attack and after finding the body that you can deal with the worst humanity has to throw at you. And on Saturday night, you had the wherewithal to rescue this wretched man's dog.

That gives you brownie points in my book. I'm not sure that following a violent criminal shows good judgement but your instincts were correct. Time will tell whether you're a team player."

"But Gary helped on Saturday night. He's been a good partner."

Was there something in Sara's eyes? A trace of doubt, perhaps.

"What is it?" Fiona asked.

"Nothing, Ma'am." She shook her head. "Would I need to formally apply, attend an interview, and everything else?"

"I've already cleared the secondment with the super if you want it, and then we'll see if you are a good fit and if you're interested in applying for a permanent position yes, you will have to fill out an application form and go through the formal process."

Carlos grinned. His lip was almost back to normal.

"Can I just ask something, Ma'am?"

"Go ahead."

"Am I being offered this on merit, or because I'm a black woman?"

"Legitimate question," said Fiona, "but not one you should ask me. I don't operate like that. I won't say I didn't use those facts to persuade the super to provide funding for an extra DC were you to apply in the near future." Fiona had employed all the politically correct terms to get her way with Superintendent Henley. "But that's not why I'm offering you the job. If you don't believe me, don't accept it."

Carlos looked at Sara. "Fiona isn't that type. She wouldn't offer you a job to fill a quota. In fact, she'd rail against it if anyone tried to make her take someone she didn't deem suitable. She's one of the most politically incorrect people I know. If she's offering you a job, Sara, it's because she believes you're good enough."

Sara seemed to grow another few inches under the praise. She and Carlos seemed to have bonded.

"I'll need to think about it, Ma'am, if that's okay?"

"Of course you will, because you'll be joining the serious crime squad, and if you think you've met danger out there on the streets, you've no idea what you're gonna come across as a member of my team. Your mum might be about to get a lot more worried."

"Thanks for the heads-up, Ma'am, and for the offer."

"Okay, I need to speak to Jacobi in private now. I look forward to hearing from you."

After Sara left, Carlos eyed her. *Please don't be sympathetic;* she wasn't sure if she could hold herself together if he went all soppy on her.

"I gave you my house keys as a gift, and you say you're homeless."

"Oh, stop your moaning, Carlos. There's not a lot wrong with you; you're back to your normal, irritating self. Now we've got work to do."

Carlos laughed, but his hand immediately went to his ribs.

"Well, almost back to normal," Fiona forced a chuckle.

20

Carlos's heart went out to Fiona. As if she hadn't had enough trauma. Now it looked like a man she respected and confided in, and whom Carlos believed she was attracted to, might be mixed up with the criminals they were chasing. "Sorry about Paul, Fiona. I know you like the guy."

Fiona didn't reply. Instead, she drained the final dregs of coffee from her mug, ignoring the issue. He understood why. She intertwined her fingers and stretched them out until they cracked.

"How did your meeting go with your DCI?"

Eventually, she spoke. "Flatley didn't show. I think Superintendent Henley might have been considering taking me off the case after the boat episode. She didn't say as much, but why else wouldn't he be there? It's a good thing we're short-staffed, but she made it clear she wants results, although we have to tread carefully with Michael Kingsland. He's a friend, and he has more friends in high places."

"That doesn't surprise me," Carlos said, trying not to sound cynical. "So, what next?"

"We have to get on with this investigation. Give me the registration numbers that Sara mentioned." He noticed she didn't ask for the photos of Tyson with Paul, but he knew she would when she was ready. Carlos handed her a sheet of paper.

Fiona phoned her sergeant. "Hugh, I'm going to email you some car registrations. The owners might be persons of interest. Can you get a trace and let me know if the owners have criminal records? Then I need everything on a guy named Tyson Jerome, check the PNC and H.O.L.M.E.S, see if he's been on our radar before. Let me know what you find. We'll have a briefing at 2 p.m. okay?"

Carlos could tell Fiona was in no mood for tea and sympathy, so when she finished her call, he looked up and asked. "What do you suggest we do next?"

"As I've been warned off Kingsland, he'll have to wait. We'll pay a visit to Foxdale Baptist and a certain Paul Allen."

"Is that wise, Fiona? Do you really want to show our hand this early? Isn't it better to keep what we know under wraps for now and allow things to develop? It would be better not to let Paul know we're onto him."

"We don't know he's involved, Carlos," she snapped.

"We don't," he said patiently, "but whether he is or he isn't, he's now a suspect, and with all due respect, you are personally involved. I suggest we behave as if nothing's happened."

Fiona's face flushed scarlet, her eyes threatening rage. "I

can't continue as if nothing's happened without additional context or information."

Carlos recognised the look of anger and despair in Fiona's eyes. The feeling that she'd been manipulated would be the most painful thing to bear. All this on top of the anguish she must be suffering about losing her boat. It was a tough ask. But if she went to see Paul in this state, she would say all the wrong things. He trusted her implicitly, but right now her emotions were running too high.

"Fiona. You're the ultimate professional. You can do this. How about you call him and ask if he's arranged that meeting with Princess?"

With fists clenched in her lap, she snapped. "You do it."

"Okay," Carlos agreed. "Give me his number."

Carlos called Paul, keeping his phone on speaker, hoping that Fiona could control herself enough to stay silent. The cheerful voice of Paul Allen answered.

"Hello, this is Pastor Allen. How can I help?"

"Hi Paul, it's Carlos Jacobi."

"Good to hear from you, Carlos. How's your investigation?"

"We're following several leads." Carlos noticed Fiona shaking her head vigorously, but he wouldn't be telling the pastor anything, knowing what he did about the man's meeting with Tyson Jerome.

"And how's Fiona?"

"Fiona's fine. She's busy, but she's asked me to call and see if you've managed to contact Princess."

"Almost. I got a number this morning and I've just left a message for her to ring me. As soon as she calls, I'll set something up. I suspect she'll only come here, and I think she'll want me present."

Carlos watched Fiona frantically shake her head again.

"We'll go along with whatever Princess wants," said Carlos, noting Fiona's blazing eyes boring into his. "We just need to speak to her. She might need our protection."

"Do you really think she's next on the list of this man Nicolae, who Fiona's looking for?"

Fiona's head shot up, and she mouthed to Carlos. "I didn't mention his name."

"I'm surprised Fiona gave you that name," said Carlos innocently.

"I already knew his name," Paul said. "I didn't enjoy deceiving Fiona, but I explained to her I have to be cautious in order to help get those who want to get off the streets and into safety."

"It must be hard to find the balance," said Carlos. "If you know about Nicolae, he might try to bribe you."

Fiona's eyes were wide with warning.

"Where are you going with this, Carlos?" asked Paul, sounding defensive. Fiona made a finger-slashing motion across her neck, signalling he shouldn't continue.

"I'm sorry, Paul. I'm always in private investigator mode, and I sometimes ask silly questions. We're really grateful for your help on this. If you could let me know as soon as you've arranged the meeting, I'll grab Fiona and we'll come over."

"Wouldn't it be better for me to call her?"

"She's in and out of meetings all day, which is why she asked me to call."

"Are you making progress with the leads you're following?" Paul asked.

"It's slow going at the minute," Carlos replied. "All sorts of curveballs heading our way. But we'll get there. Whoever's committing these crimes, we'll find them. Fiona will arrest them, and they will be taken off the streets of Leicester. I can assure you of that."

"I like your determination," said Paul. "I'll be in touch as soon as I hear from Princess."

"Look forward to hearing from you," said Carlos, ending the call.

"Well, isn't he the smooth one? He's protecting someone," Fiona said through gritted teeth. "He's lying. I didn't tell him Nicolae's name, and I don't believe he would have known it before, unless he's in league with him."

"You said Nicolae might have a plant in a church. It wouldn't be the first time." Carlos remembered the charismatic priest who had been involved in dirty dealings when they finally caught DCI Terry Masters. "I just didn't expect it to be Paul; he seems so genuine."

"How much does he know and how deep in is he?" Fiona said. "Those are the questions I want answers to. And how did I fall for his claptrap?"

"As you say," Carlos said, "he's smooth, and he had us both fooled. We'll need to be careful how we speak to him. You're going to have to keep your emotions under control before we speak to him."

"Don't worry, he already thinks I'm an emotional wreck. I'll keep playing the emotional wreck and now I've lost my home, he'll expect some anger. I've challenged him on several things, so I can't suddenly go in all nicely, nicely."

"Neither can you go in accusatory," Carlos warned.

"Says he who nearly gave us away just then."

"I took a calculated risk. Having mentioned Nicolae, he'd have been suspicious if I hadn't dug a little."

"Don't worry, Carlos. If he's guilty, I'll arrest him with a smile on my face and consider it a lucky escape."

Carlos wondered whether this might be the final straw for Fiona. Every man she trusted let her down. Her last DCI was corrupt. Her brother's partner's father was corrupt and had almost dragged Fiona into shady dealings. And now it appeared someone smarter than any of them had manipulated her.

"I'm glad you offered Sara a secondment. You know, I thought about hiring her myself if she wanted to leave the force," he said. "I know her mum wants her to get out."

Fiona chuckled for the first time since she had arrived. "Don't you dare compete. I should have got you to sign a non-competition clause. I think she will make a good DC, and if it works out, I want her on my team."

"I suspect that's where her ambition lies. She's in the force for all the right reasons. That doesn't mean I can't try."

"You wouldn't consider joining us yourself, would you?"

Carlos checked her face to see if she was serious, but her eyes told him she was. "I don't think so. I've seen the toll it took on Rachel. If she comes back to the job, she will need my support. Apart from when I'm working with you, I spend most of my time on investigations that have nothing to do with serious crime. I wouldn't want her to have the stress of worrying about me while working the job herself."

"Don't you worry about her?" Fiona asked.

"Every single day," said Carlos. "But I can't tell her that."

"Why?"

"She'd take it the wrong way and think I was being the alpha male trying to protect his woman."

"Which, of course, you are."

"Perhaps, but she would be just as protective of me. Especially if she saw my face right now. I haven't called her yet because I'd have to make a video call, and I didn't want her to see this mug of mine until it looks better. I've texted and told her I'll call tomorrow."

"Oh, I get it now."

"She'll have enough work on board the *Coral Queen* without worrying about her husband looking like he's done ten rounds in a boxing ring. Plus, she already knows Nicolae's involved, and she knows how dangerous he is. I don't want to add to her worry."

"Fair point. Well, as I can't tear Paul Allen limb from limb, perhaps I'd better ignore orders and interview Michael Kingsland."

"Won't you get into trouble?"

"Superintendent Henley told me to track Nicolae down, and she should know by now that I'm not going to back off Kingsland if speaking to him can help. I've had enough of being pushed around. Let's shake a few trees, Carlos, and see what scum we unearth."

Carlos grinned at his friend's determination. "It looks like you might be the one in need of a new job, but I'm all for shaking trees. First, let me call Sara and ask if she'll look after Lady for a couple of hours. She's nervous about me leaving her at the minute."

"Sure. Go ahead. We can drop her off on the way."

"Better idea. We'll walk and I'll buy you a burger on the way." Carlos didn't point out that Sara's friend's flat was in a pedestrianised zone and five-minutes away, because she didn't need to know the logistics, but he suspected she needed food.

21

Carlos parked his Capri in a dedicated car park facing a modern hexagonal office building with steps of privacy glass reaching right to the top floor. Michael Kingsland's base was on an industrial estate close to the Fosse Park Shopping Centre, not too far from Fiona's police headquarters on the outskirts of Leicester. A bold move from someone willing to hide in plain sight if he were a criminal.

As they climbed out of the car, Fiona whistled. "My, oh my. I wonder if he designed this place as well as his other monstrosities."

"It was certainly built in the last few years," said Carlos, "he could well have done."

"How has this man stayed off my radar?" Fiona asked. "It appears he's been investigated twice over his intimidation tactics, but no charges were ever made. Henley says it's because people are jealous of his success, but I wonder."

"He could have bought people off, I suppose, although

we should assume he's a legitimate businessman until we prove otherwise."

"He's dirty, Carlos, I can feel it in my bones. The man's gathering friends in high places for a reason. And the squeaky-clean Jodie Whitwick certainly didn't like him. That's enough for me."

Carlos laughed. "You're sounding like Rachel. Except she uses the term gut rather than bones. Are you sure Jodie Whitwick liked anyone in power?"

Fiona looked at him as he winced on closing the car door. "Are you sure you're okay?"

She had tried to persuade him to let her drive, and yesterday he would have taken her up on the offer, but he had explained that climbing in and out of her Mini would be more painful than a seatbelt rub. "I'm still taking ibuprofen recommended by the paramedic, but I've switched from codeine to paracetamol as the codeine was too strong for me. The medication takes the edge off."

"If you say so," Fiona said, her eyes filled with concern. "I've been reading all about Jodie Whitwick. I admire her tenacity, but I can see why she riled people. She saw the world in black and white with no grey areas."

"Some people are like that," Carlos replied, starting towards the entrance of *Michael Kingsland Developments Incorporated*. "How would you like to play this? Good cop, bad cop, or take it as it comes?"

"Considering I've been ordered to leave him alone, it might be best if we do good cop, good cop. I'd rather he didn't call the Chief Constable the minute we leave."

"So, what are we giving as our reason for interviewing him?" Carlos asked.

"I've been thinking about that. Let's use the fact that Jodie Whitwick implied he wasn't always on the straight and narrow and see where it leads." Fiona stopped outside the entrance, her face doubtful, as if she might change her mind and obey her superintendent.

"Good plan," Carlos said, marching through the revolving door. "Let's go."

Carlos strolled into the huge ground-floor reception with numerous business listings signposted on a board. Fiona sighed as they approached a young man in a smart grey suit sitting behind a shiny desk and showed her identity card. "Detective Inspector Fiona Cook to speak to Michael Kingsland."

"His office is on the fourth floor." The man pointed to his left. "You can take the lift, or if you prefer, the stairs--"

"The lift is fine," said Fiona, suddenly taking the lead lest Carlos drag her to the stairwell, but she needn't have worried. He wasn't up to it.

Inside the lift, Carlos said. "He didn't bat an eyelid when you said you were a detective."

"Probably thinks I'm one of Kingsland's friends," said Fiona, using her fingers to form air quotes around the word 'friends'.

"Or he just doesn't care," Carlos mused.

They exited the lift into a plush reception where they were met by a not so friendly receptionist. Fiona repeated her ID badge routine. "Detective Inspector Fiona Cook and

Private Investigator Carlos Jacobi to speak to Michael Kingsland."

"Do you have an appointment?" The woman behind the desk was in her fifties with highlighted brown hair cut into a long bob. She wore a lime green jacket over a grey dress matched with printed lime green flowers.

"Do I need one?" Fiona asked casually. "We just want to ask him a few questions."

"Mr Kingsland is a very busy man. I'll see if he's free," said the woman, grudgingly picking up the phone.

"Sorry to bother you, but there's a Detective Inspector Cook and a private investigator in reception who would like a word."

Carlos heard a man's voice on the other end of the line but couldn't make out what he was saying.

"They didn't say. Shall I ask them to make an appointment?"

Fiona tapped her fingers on the desk, glaring at the woman. "It won't take long."

Kingsland must have heard, as when the receptionist put the phone down, she sounded more amenable. "Take a seat. Mr Kingsland will be with you shortly."

While Fiona stomped over and helped herself to water from a water dispenser before stomping over to sit on one of a row of cushioned chairs, Carlos stayed put, going on a charm offensive.

"This is an amazing building. It must be nice working here."

The receptionist forced a smile.

Carlos persevered. "When you work for a talented and

philanthropic developer like Mr Kingsland, I'm not surprised. Did he design this building himself?" His tactic worked.

"Yes, Mr Kingsland is amazing. He does more of the buying and selling and leaves the planning to his architects, although he sketches out designs of what he has in mind. Once the designs are in place, Mr Kingsland offers a few suggestions and requests tweaks before applying for planning permission. He's done a lot of good in this city."

"I've heard," said Carlos, still standing at the desk.

He was about to delve further when a tall man in his mid-forties with wavy brown hair and a close-cut beard opened a door off to the side. He wore a designer suit, a striped tie and gleaming black shoes. The shoeshine would have gone down well in the army.

"Are you DI Cook?" he looked at Carlos.

"No, I'm Carlos Jacobi, a private detective. That's Detective Inspector Cook," Carlos pointed to his friend.

Fiona rose from the chair where she'd been pretending to leaf through a magazine, but no doubt listening to Carlos and the receptionist's conversation. Kingsland held out his hand. Carlos shook it firmly. Fiona's handshake seemed more reluctant.

"What can I do for you, Inspector?"

"Can we do this privately?" Fiona said, giving the receptionist another glare.

Kingsland looked at his watch. "I have a meeting in fifteen minutes."

"This won't take long," Fiona said. "Just a matter of routine, and we appreciate you seeing us, sir." Carlos was impressed with her remembering to keep to the good cop routine. Under the circumstances, it went against her instincts, but she had to keep it genial. That they were there at all meant Fiona was skating on thin ice.

Kingsland relaxed. "Why don't we go through to my office? I'm sorry I can't offer you hot drinks, but I'm pressed for time."

"That's okay, I've had water," said Fiona, tossing the paper cup into a recycling bin.

They followed Kingsland along a wide corridor lined with offices. Carlos glanced at people on their phones or staring at computers. One of the rooms must have been a meeting room because there was a modelled 3D building design on top of a rectangular table. Carlos wondered if that was the one Kingsland was trying to get planning permission for.

Kingsland opened a door leading to a spacious office. "In here."

As they entered, Carlos was drawn to the view. A floor to ceiling window overlooked an outside area in the centre of the uniquely designed building. A fountain cascaded into a pool containing large koi carp in the centre of a paved area. The perimeter contained a lawn, a couple of exotic trees with large green leaves, and a variety of flowering shrubs. Modern benches gave it a park vibe.

"What a beautiful outlook," Carlos remarked.

"I like it," said Kingsland. "Did you say you're a private investigator?"

"Yes, I'm working alongside the serious crimes unit on a triple murder investigation."

Kingsland raised a manicured eyebrow, revealing dark blue eyes that lacked warmth. He studied Carlos, a puzzled expression on his face as he took a seat behind his enormous, minimalist desk. The size of the desk and the positioning of his chair were designed to make whoever entered the office feel inferior, thought Carlos.

"Please take a seat." He waved to two chairs on the other side of the desk, deliberately positioned to be lower than his own. If Fiona sat in one, it would have the desired effect, but she didn't.

"As you have little time, Mr Kingsland, I'll stand and come straight to the point," she said. "I've been sitting for most of the morning. It's good to stretch the legs." Having made it clear she wasn't playing Kingsland's psychological game; Fiona strolled over to the window behind Kingsland, looking anything but inferior as she pretended to gaze out on the exterior.

"So, how can I help?" asked Kingsland tersely.

"Would you mind telling us about your relationship with the late councillor, Jodie Whitwick?" Fiona said.

A brief flicker of a frown crossed Kingsland's eyes before disappearing again. "It's no secret that Mrs Whitwick and I didn't see eye to eye, but I was sorry to hear of her death. As I'm sure many people in the city were."

"Not as many as you might imagine," said Fiona.

Kingsland tried hard to hide a smirk. "It doesn't always pay to make enemies. Jodie Whitwick believed what she believed, and sadly, one of the minority groups that she detested so much took revenge. People can only be pushed so far."

"Is that what you think happened?" Fiona asked.

"From what I read in the newspaper article on Friday night, it looks that way."

"I take it you missed the part of the spread highlighting your relationship, or lack of, with the deceased?" Fiona was leaning dangerously towards bad cop.

Kingsland pursed his lips before replying. "I read that too, but that's how these people sell newspapers. As I've said, it's no secret that Mrs Whitwick and I weren't friends. The lady opposed progress and was unfortunately stuck in the past. If it had been left to her, this city wouldn't be the thriving community we have today." He steepled his hands on his desk, looking at Carlos as Fiona remained behind him.

"I take it you're the future Mrs Whitwick, opposed?" Fiona remarked, still facing the view below.

"I have grand plans for the city's future, so in that sense, yes, I am."

"So we understand," Carlos said, cutting Fiona off before she pushed too hard. "Can I ask what you think would have happened at the next planning meeting had Jodie Whitwick still been alive?"

"I see where you're going with this, Mr Jacobi. My plans would have been approved in the end; they always are."

"Why is that?" Fiona asked, moving back into Kingsland's line of sight.

"Common sense always prevails in the end. Sometimes it takes time for people to get there."

"Would you admit that Jodie Whitwick's opposition to your proposals had become a thorn in your side?" Carlos did a little pushing of his own.

"Her opposition wasn't helpful, but most councillors are in favour. There are a few opposing groups, of course, but there are always those who don't want major developments in their backyard. The 'anywhere but here brigade'. How are we supposed to build the houses the country needs, and the government wants, without ruffling a few feathers? What people like Mrs Whitwick don't understand is that there are only so many square metres on our small island. Leicester's a big city and can take it."

"How much of Leicester do you own, Mr Kingsland?" Fiona asked,

"I don't think that applies to your inquiries, but it's a matter of public record. I own twelve commercial units and twenty residential estates. Others, we build and sell on, but the majority, we rent out."

"How valuable is the proposed project?" Carlos quizzed.

"Again, it's all in the planning records. Once built, it will be worth something in the region of..." He waved his hand in the air. "Let's say a billion pounds, something like that."

Even Carlos raised his eyebrows at the figure.

"And you believe your planning would have gone ahead on Thursday night with or without Mrs Whitwick?" Fiona asked, her tone sarcastic.

"I had assurances it would, but even if it hadn't, we'd have gone through a few tweaks and begun the process again. We also have the option of appealing to a higher authority."

Fiona paced the office, and Carlos could see how she pressed her lips tight, trying to stop herself from firing tougher questions at the smug property developer. He was the kind of man who riled her. A man in power and not afraid to abuse it, Carlos suspected.

"Not all of your proposals pass, do they?" Fiona said. "Jodie Whitwick stopped at least four in the past. Didn't they become community projects?"

Kingsland's eyes darkened as he met Fiona's challenge. This was clearly a man who didn't like being tested, and definitely not one who liked to lose. He stood up, shrugging his shoulders. "You win some, you lose some, detective. Now, is there anything specific you want to ask me before you leave?" He looked at his watch again. A Rolex, Carlos noted.

"Can I ask you a question, Mr Kingsland?" Carlos stood as if to leave. "Do you employ a protection detail?"

Kingsland took a step back but recovered. "Most men in my position employ people to manage their safety, Mr Jacobi."

"That's a yes then," Carlos suggested,

"I have a small protection team."

"How small?" asked Fiona, jumping on the lead Carlos was following.

He waved his hand again, making it obvious this was his way of avoiding awkward questions. "There are six on the team."

Carlos did the maths: four at his place, one at Fiona's, and one to protect Kingsland. "Would it be possible for us to have a word with them?"

"I don't understand why you want to do that," Kingsland said.

"We'd just like to make sure they haven't been overeager

in their protection duties," said Fiona. "You know, perhaps doing things you might not know about."

"Such as?"

Carlos shook his head at Fiona. He didn't want her to mention their attack. She took the warning.

"We would just like to rule them out of our inquiries regarding Jodie Whitwick. You're quite right. It looks as if a minority group attacked and murdered her. But with the amount of public interest in her death, we have to be seen to be following all lines of inquiry. As your name cropped up as somebody who she wasn't – how shall I say – fond of, we just want to cross you and your men off our list."

Kingsland visibly relaxed, adjusting his gold cufflinks. *Who wears cufflinks these days?*

"So, is it possible to speak to them?" Fiona pressed.

"If it helps you tick a box, I can make them available to you," said Kingsland, his grin smug.

"We appreciate your time. Mr Kingsland, and apologise for any inconvenience. I hope we haven't disrupted your day too much." Only Carlos would recognise how insincere Fiona was as she pasted on a smile.

Kingsland's smile was also false. Carlos wanted to punch him in the face, convinced he'd given the order for what had happened to them. As if rubbing it in, Kingsland grew in confidence, eyeing Carlos closely. "Have you been in a fight, Mr Jacobi?"

"He's an amateur boxer, aren't you, Carlos? As you can see, he's not that good," Fiona said with a chuckle. "Thanks again for your time, sir."

"You're welcome, Inspector. I'll ask the manager of my security detail to call you. How will he contact you?"

"Are they not in the building?" Carlos challenged.

"I don't need protection here. We've got reception downstairs and I've got Priscilla on the desk."

"Yes, I can imagine she would drive any dark forces away, but you must have them ready for when you leave the office?" Carlos persisted.

Kingsland sighed. "They have an office on the ground floor."

"In that case, the quicker we speak to them, the quicker we can tick our box sir," said Fiona.

"I'll ask Priscilla to let them know you're on your way. She'll give you directions."

"Thank you," said Carlos. "It will save us an extra journey."

"I'll walk you out and speak to Priscilla," Kingsland said. When they got to the front desk, Kingsland had a mumbled conversation with Priscilla. "That's organised. Good luck with your investigation, DI Cook, Mr Jacobi."

Carlos was certain that most of the security detail would have disappeared before they arrived downstairs, but he and Fiona had made their point. Kingsland left them with Priscilla as if he didn't care, but the clammy hand Carlos shook said otherwise.

22

"That was a complete waste of time," Fiona complained once she and Carlos left *Michael Kingsland Developments Incorporated.*

"We showed he's on our radar; that's the important thing," Carlos said. "The fact that he warned any minders we'd be able to identify proves it. I'd recognise the voice of the guy who threatened me just as Sara recognised the eyes of the man who attacked her. I think we can be certain Kingsland dished out the orders to frighten us. What we don't know is whether his goons went too far. I'm sure one would be walking with a limp after the kick I gave him."

"Were you wearing those big boots of yours?"

"Yep. I'd planned to take Lady out once I got back, but of course that never happened. Would you recognise the voice of the guy who threatened you?"

"Not only his voice," said Fiona, "the odour. He reeked of cigar smoke and a cheap cologne that must have been a gift from his mother."

When they got in the car, Carlos's phone rang. "It's Paul," he showed Fiona the screen and put the phone on speaker.

Twenty minutes later, Carlos parked outside the now-familiar Foxdale Baptist Church. Fiona's tight-lipped glare told him everything. It would be hard for her to control her temper. Plus, the burger she ate hours ago must be wearing off, which didn't bode well for the upcoming meeting.

Carlos's ribs felt less painful when he climbed out of the car. The painkillers must be working. Paul was waiting outside for them. He strolled towards them, beaming at Fiona.

Fiona just about managed a curt nod. Paul's jaw dropped when he looked at Carlos.

"What happened to you?"

"I had an unwelcome visit from four men after leaving here on Saturday night. They warned me not to investigate anymore."

Paul's eyes seemed genuinely concerned. "That's terrible."

"What was really terrible is they took his dog," Fiona snapped. "They would have killed her if one of my officers hadn't rescued her."

Paul was a great actor, or he genuinely knew nothing about the events. "Where is she? Is she okay?"

"Yes," said Carlos. "An off-duty police officer recognised her and stepped in."

"You must have been devastated."

Carlos headed towards the building, reliving the pain that had threatened to overwhelm him when he thought he'd lost his beloved dog. "You could say that," he replied. "But I'd rather not think about it. Fiona wasn't spared either. They burned her boat to ashes."

The concern on Paul's face again appeared genuine when he looked at Fiona. "Why would anyone do such a thing?"

"Evil people do evil things," Fiona replied sharply, "as I told you that night. Like Carlos, I'd rather not talk about it. Where is this woman?"

"She's in the annexe. I persuaded her to come in on the basis that her life might be in danger. I realise you've gone through terrible trauma yourselves, but please be careful. She's terrified."

"Fine, we'll let you know when we're done," said Fiona, marching towards the annexe.

Paul hurried after her. "She won't see you without me."

"You realise this is confidential police business, and I could just take her to the station?" Fiona snapped again.

Carlos caught her arm. "We agreed we'd do it her way, Fiona. Let's just do as she wishes. If she wants Paul to be present, it's fine. He's a man of principle." The word choked in his throat as it came out. "Anything we say will be confidential, you understand that, Paul?"

"Of course," Paul replied. "I've reassured you on that score, Fiona. Nothing you say leaves these premises."

"It's who enters these premises I'm more concerned about," said Fiona.

Paul's brow furrowed; he looked slightly confused.

"I told you, the likes of Travis don't change, and I'm still certain you've got a mole in your congregation."

"Let's leave that conversation until afterwards. I think

the sooner we see Princess and put her mind at rest, the better. Otherwise, she'll run."

"Do you know where she's staying?" asked Carlos.

"I can't answer that," Paul said.

"This is a murder investigation, Pastor." Fiona stated, leaving Paul nonplussed as she stormed off towards the annexe.

A smartly dressed woman greeted them, challenging Carlos's assumptions about the person they expected to meet. This woman gave the impression of someone working in a professional position. She could easily be a businesswoman.

"Princess, these are the people I told you about: Detective Inspector Fiona Cook and Carlos Jacobi. They would like to ask you some questions."

Despite. Paul's insistence that Princess wanted him present, she didn't look for one moment like the weak and feeble type who would need a chaperone. Fiona must have got the same impression because she went straight for the jugular.

"Would you be happy to speak to Carlos and me without Pastor Allen? We'd like to keep our conversation between ourselves."

Paul didn't seem happy with the question, but said nothing, allowing Princess to answer.

"I don't mind him being here."

"It would be better if we spoke to you alone," persisted Fiona.

Carlos couldn't miss the pained look crossing Paul's face.

"That's fine," Princess replied.

"Thank you, Pastor Allen," Fiona said dismissively. "We'll let you know when we've finished our interview."

Fiona had won this battle, and Paul knew it. He nodded before leaving them.

Carlos and Fiona sat down around a glass-topped table, and Princess joined them.

"We were sorry to hear about the loss of your friends," Carlos said.

"I knew Angel, but I didn't know Diane that well. I'd met her in the past but didn't know her well."

"We understand you know Ruby," Fiona said.

"Yes, but I haven't spoken to her since Angel died."

"Is Ruby correct in believing that you're now under the protection of one of the establishments where sex is sold?" Fiona asked.

"What's that got to do with this?"

"Nothing at all." Carlos shot Fiona a warning look. "We're not here to arrest you, but we are wondering whether you can tell us anything about a Mr Cross?"

"Mr Cross was nice. I can imagine what you think about men like him, but he was good to me. He put me in a decent place."

"Didn't he get you hooked on drugs?" Fiona challenged. Carlos felt the anger at Paul Allen still simmering below the surface.

"No, he never did. He gave me a choice and told me that if I was willing to entertain friends of his who had certain needs, I'd be well paid, and he'd make sure I was looked after."

Carlos and Fiona exchanged confused looks.

"So hang on," Fiona said. "You never got involved in the drug scene?"

"I would never do drugs. My parents were very strict about that."

Carlos nudged Fiona under the table with his foot, warning her not to alienate the woman. "We understood you knew Travis?" Carlos said.

"Yes. He kept quiet about my not doing drugs. I saw what addiction did to the other girls. Angel was different; she said they helped her, at least at first."

"What if you hadn't been willing to go along with Mr Cross's plans? Would he have tried to get you addicted?" Fiona scratched her head.

Princess shook her head. "No. He was in love with me. We had to be careful because he answered to someone higher, but he still protected me. He also protected Angel; we were his girls. I know there were others; maybe Diamond was one. But some weren't as well protected."

"So Mr Cross had his favourites," Carlos suggested.

"When you put it like that, I guess he did, and I was at the top of that list."

"You mentioned he answered to somebody else. Do you know who that was?"

"I don't know his name, but I saw him a few times."

Carlos leaned forward in his chair. "Can you describe him?"

"He always wore a cream suit. Jet black hair. He had an Eastern European accent, the same as Ruby's. He was suave, but with a threatening undertone. I wouldn't have wanted him as a punter. Anytime he visited, Mr Cross told me to hide in another room and not to let the man know I was there. But I listened. And after a couple of times, I peeped through a crack in the door. Mr Cross was always agitated after the man left."

"You say you listened," said Fiona. "Can you recall any of the conversations?"

"Most of the talk was boring, like code. Occasionally it was about money and quotas. And then there was a demand for Mr Cross to get more women for businessmen. It sounded like he brought some women in from abroad for the average punters. But he wanted higher-class, decent ones for others."

"The men you, Angel, Diane, and Ruby met, you mean?" Fiona asked.

"Most of the ones Angel, Ruby, and I met were overseas businessmen."

"Did you hear any other names?" Carlos asked.

"The last time the man in the cream suit came, before Mr Cross disappeared, he mentioned a woman who was giving one of his clients trouble."

Jodie Whitwick, Carlos thought.

"I think it was the woman who was found dead last week. This guy wanted Mr Cross to do something – I didn't hear what, but Mr Cross refused. The man threatened him."

"Did you hear the man threaten him?" Fiona asked.

"No, but I could tell from the way he behaved afterwards. He was nervous, terrified in fact. That's when he packed his bags. He didn't tell me he was leaving, but he told me to warn Angel, Diamond, and Ruby that they would have to fend for themselves. He said the flat he'd put me in belonged to him and he'd bought it with cash. Nobody knew about it. He'd always told me never to meet punters there, so I met them in posh hotels. That's why I'm safe."

"Does Pastor Allen know where your flat is?" Carlos asked.

"He's the only one who does. I'm not telling you where it is. As long as I'm there, I feel safe. I'm not doing that kind of work anymore. Mr Cross told me to get out of sex work and that he would take care of me. I receive monthly deposits into my bank account."

Carlos and Fiona exchange glances.

"From Mr Cross?" Fiona asked.

Princess nodded.

So he's alive, thought Carlos. "We would really like to speak to him, Princess. Do you have any idea where he is?"

"No, and even if I did, I wouldn't tell you. His phone is no longer active."

"Would you allow us to examine the bank account details?" Fiona tried a different angle.

"No way," said Princess.

Carlos could feel Fiona about to argue, but shook his head. They could do it without Princess having to know about it. It would be safer all round.

"Paul said you think I'm in danger. How can I be?"

"We believe the man Mr Cross met regularly is now cleaning up after Mr Cross. He appears to be getting rid of anyone he thinks was treated differently. This man is dangerous, and he doesn't like loose ends."

"So why isn't Ruby in danger?" Princess asked.

Good question, thought Carlos. Could Ruby be working

for Nicolae? She clearly didn't know where Princess had got to. Was she working with Paul as well? "We believe you may be next on his list. He's making it look as if the dead women are being killed by a religious fanatic. I'm afraid that's the way he works," Carlos continued. "He uses distraction and confusion."

"There's one more facade of the clock tower where a body hasn't been found," Fiona added. "This man knows that a serial killer is ritualistic and so far, he's planted bodies anticlockwise. One more would finish the circle."

"You think he's after me because I knew Mr Cross?" Princess seemed startled by the revelation.

"That depends on how good Mr Cross was at protecting you. If he was as good as you think he was, they might not find you."

"So he could go after Ruby," Princess said. "I should warn her."

"I think it's best if nobody knows where you are. Leave Ruby to us," said Carlos.

"Are you absolutely certain that this man didn't know of your existence?" Fiona asked.

"Positive. Only Ruby and Travis know about me. Mr Cross kept records of all his girls and their addresses. That man had a copy. But Mr Cross told me he would never give him my details. Now I wonder if my jobs were separate from the overall operation. Mr Cross may have pocketed that money for himself. Keeping the slime bag in the cream suit out of it entirely."

"That's plausible," said Fiona to Carlos before looking at

Princess. "I'm willing to speak to people about witness protection if you want it?"

"No, I've got the flat. I received the deeds about a month ago with an owner change. It's mine now. But after what you've said, I might sell it and move out of Leicester. Because I don't need to do this work anymore, I could go somewhere else and live off the money that comes into my bank every month or from the proceeds of the flat."

"As long as the man in the cream suit doesn't find out where Mr Cross has run to," Fiona warned.

"The cream suit slimeball thought he knew everything, but Mr Cross was cleverer than him. I think he always had an exit plan. I believe if he'd had more time, he'd have taken me with him."

"And you think it's too risky for him to get in contact with you now?" Carlos checked.

Princess seemed sad but philosophical. "That's just about the sum of it, but I'm fine on my own."

"If you need help." Carlos handed her his card. "Call me on that number, day or night. We don't need to know where you are now, but if you need me, I'll be there."

"Okay, but it sounds like you need to make sure nothing happens to Ruby," Princess said. "I've got a new phone and Paul's the only one who has the number."

"Leave that with us," Fiona said.

Carlos leaned back in the chair after Princess left. "That was enlightening. Paul said he only got her number this morning. Why lie?"

"And who else might he give it to?" Fiona said sullenly, "We already know Paul's a lying scumbag, but I don't think he'd dare give the number away when we've just seen her. We'll deal with him later. For now, we need to work out whether Ruby is playing both sides."

"Nicolae always has people close to the action. I suggest you pick Ruby up later, and this time we have a formal chat," Carlos suggested. "Why don't I speak to Paul now. I can pick up Lady afterwards."

"What about the briefing at two? Don't you want to come?"

"Not this time," Carlos said.

"Can I take your car?"

"Have you not heard of Uber?"

"Don't worry about it, I'll make some calls now about Michael Kingsland's protection team and ask uniform to pick up Ruby. I'll get someone to pick me up in a patrol car. Are you sure you don't want me to talk to Paul?" Fiona's eyes blazed with fire.

"Maybe later if I don't get anywhere," Carlos said.

23

Paul looked up from his notes as Carlos knocked on his office door. He waved a hand, inviting Carlos inside.

"No Fiona?" he asked.

"She needs to make a few calls, and then she's got a briefing at the station. A patrol car will collect her. I need to get my dog from the person looking after her."

"So what was that all about? Fiona's angry with me about something, but I don't know what I've done."

Carlos looked at Paul, weighing up whether to say anything at all. "She's angry with the world at the minute. She's lost her home, Paul. On top of that, she's investigating a triple homicide and trying to prevent a fourth murder. That's a lot on one woman's plate; please give her a little latitude."

"You're right, and I'm so sorry about her boat. It's just that I thought we were friends. I'd like to help her if I can. She's suffering, Carlos."

Carlos looked the pastor in the eyes. If this guy was bad, he was an incredible actor. "Nobody else has a number for Princess apart from you. Why did you tell me this morning that you only just got her number?"

"I'm sorry, but I too am juggling multiple things at the minute, Carlos. Trust goes both ways, and right now I'm not sure who I can rely on. Fiona told me I might have a mole in my congregation, so I'm looking at everybody through suspicious eyes, which really isn't doing me any favours as a pastor."

"Fiona and I are used to suspecting everyone, even those close to us, but I understand why you don't want to. My wife's father is a vicar. I'm not sure if I mentioned that before."

"Then you'll understand the fine line I have to tread while working on a troubled estate. On the one hand, I want people to come in, people from every background. But I don't want to feel we are being used as a crime hub."

"Do you think you might be?"

Paul looked over Carlos's shoulder to check that the outside corridor was clear. He got up and closed the door. "Ever since Fiona told me she thought I might have a spy in my congregation, I've been uptight. I did some digging and looked at all the people who have joined the church in the last six months. I've also checked the people running groups, and the ones who attend services or groups regularly versus the ones who just show up occasionally. Of course people come and go in every church, and on an estate like this one, I've expected the fluidity. Some show up irregularly, while some are committed. Some you get to know really well; others you hardly ever know at all. But I've been suspicious of a group that meets on ad hoc Monday mornings."

"Did this group meet this morning?" Carlos asked.

Paul nodded. "To be honest, I've got a bad feeling about them. It's not just because they're all male – they call it a working man's brunch – but there's something menacing about them. At first, I took them at face value and didn't object to the fact that they like to get together in a safe and warm environment where they can eat and talk."

"But you don't believe that is what they're doing?"

"Oh, I'm pretty sure they're talking things through. It's what they might talk through that concerns me." Paul seemed momentarily lost; a look of despair crossed his face as he rubbed his beard.

"What makes you think now that their meeting is suspicious? Surely you have similar groups."

"It's the guy who leads. He's from out of the area and always calls an hour before they want to meet. He doesn't strike me as a do-good type. When he shows up, he comes to my office, laughs and jokes briefly, and then joins the others in the annexe. He pays me fifty pounds for the use of the annexe when I only charge twenty pounds an hour. When he arrived this morning, I kept him longer than usual and engaged him in a more normal conversation."

"And?" Carlos asked.

"We chatted about Nottingham, where he told me he had family. He said his sister, mum and dad all lived that way, but he lived in Leicester. He was cagey about where. I suggested I might facilitate the group sometimes with free counselling. He just laughed and told me to my face it definitely wasn't that sort of meeting. He said it was more of a planning meeting. That's when my ears pricked up, and I wondered if he and these others might be involved in the unrest you and Fiona think is being orchestrated. When he stood up, I moved closer to him, noticing he'd undone his coat. I had the heating on high because an hour before I'd had an elderly lady in who feels the cold and had forgotten to turn it down. That's when I noticed a bulge in his right jeans pocket. He removed a fifty-pound note from a bundle."

"I see."

"It looked like a bundle of money. I deliberately walked him out of the office, taking my time to shake his hand and try to get a peek at the money. Thing is, Carlos, my dilemma is that I don't know what to do about it. I can't suddenly tell them they can't meet here because they might be genuine. They could be builders getting together to talk about their next project, or any other tradesmen for that matter."

Carlos could see from Paul's face how conflicted he was. "But you think they are up to no good?"

"That's why I wanted to speak to Fiona. I was hoping to stay in the meeting and talk to her afterwards, but she railroaded me out as if I were a suspect."

"Now that you mention it." Carlos said.

Hurt filled Paul's eyes as they widened. "She can't think for a minute that I would have anything to do with burning down her boat or having you beaten to a pulp, surely?"

"The thing is, Paul, Fiona trusts – trusted you, and her

trust doesn't come easily. All I can say is that you were seen with this guy this morning."

"Tyson?"

"Yes, at least he's using his real name," said Carlos. "This Tyson is involved in the riots. He shoved a broken bottle into the head of a young police officer. That officer needed eighteen stitches. And then, on her way to stay with a friend, she found Jodie Whitwick's body."

"Oh, no," Paul rubbed his forehead. "I can't have a man like that holding meetings here. I'll take anyone from any background as long as they're willing to change, but I will not have the building used in this way."

"Hold fire on that until I've spoken to Fiona. Because if we don't get any further with our investigation, we might need to set up surveillance of their next meeting. When was the last time they met before today?"

"Last Tuesday."

"The night of the last riot."

"Why have they chosen to meet here?"

"Because you're a pillar of the local community," said Carlos. "Nobody's going to suspect anyone coming here of being up to no good. And also, if they are not from this estate, which I suspect they are not, they won't be recognised. Can you describe these men?"

"Not really. They park in the car park and go into the annexe while Tyson comes in here and pays me for the use of the room. We usually pass the time of day; then he joins them, and they disappear an hour later. I watched them leave at lunchtime and noticed one of them was limping."

Carlos's hand went to his ribs; his eyes shot up. "Was the limp new? Which leg?"

"I think so. They all seem fairly fit usually, and I'd not noticed anyone limping before, but I couldn't swear to it. It was his right leg he was having problems with. Now I think about it, he's the only one that I recognise out of the group because I've seen him at functions."

"What functions?"

"City functions involving business people. The police commissioner and members of PCCs all attend. We get together and discuss how we can improve the community."

"And what's this guy's role?" Carlos asked, though he already knew the answer.

"He's some sort of bodyguard for a city developer, which is why I initially had them down as builders." Paul scratched his head. "What's the guy's name now? He's often in the news."

"Michael Kingsland," said Carlos.

"Yes, that's him. The man with the limp works for him."

Carlos felt his heart turn to stone as he gripped the arms of the chair.

"Are you okay, Carlos?"

"He's one of the men who jumped me. I got a kick in, which is where he got the limp."

"He could have the limp from anywhere. He might have got it playing football," said Paul.

"I don't do coincidences, Paul. And from what you're telling me about these guys; they are involved in nasty stuff. I believe most of these men work for Michael Kingsland, but Tyson works for Nicolae."

Paul's face turned ashen.

"I have to ask you, Paul. How did you really get the name Nicolae? I know for a fact Fiona didn't tell you and she doesn't believe you were aware of it before."

Paul's hands splayed across his desk, fiddling with papers. "This is between you, me and Fiona. A member of my congregation used to be involved in the sex trade. She got out years ago. I won't name her even if you arrest me. She keeps in touch with Mr Cross, who Travis mentioned to you."

"Boy, that man certainly has a loyal following of women," Carlos said.

"You're referring to Princess," said Paul. "He's looked after her, Carlos."

"Yeah, she said. So how does this woman keep in touch with a man we badly need to speak to?"

"He has a burner phone, but she'd never give you the number."

"Why would he keep in touch with this member of your congregation? Is she another one who thinks he's in love with her?"

"She's his mother, Carlos, but nobody knows that, and I'd like to keep it that way. I asked her to get the name of the man Fiona is looking for. I was trying to help."

"I don't suppose you got her to find out where Nicolae is, because he's as slippery as an eel. People rarely see him."

"So I hear. Mr Cross doesn't know where Nicolae is, and his mother's changed her name. He never wants her to mention Nicolae again."

"You could have just told me all this when I phoned you," said Carlos.

"I know, and I should have done that, but I'm feeling pretty jumpy at the minute. Can you arrest those guys so I won't have to have them in my building anymore?"

"Unfortunately, we have nothing concrete against them yet, but we will now that we know who they are. One of them burned Fiona's boat. So believe me, if anybody wants to see them behind bars when they were going to kill my dog, threaten my wife and beat me up, and after what they did to Fiona, we'll get them."

"I'll do anything I can to help apart from betraying confidences," Paul said.

"I'll pass on what you've told me to Fiona."

"She didn't really suspect me, did she?" Paul asked, his eyes misting over.

Not knowing where the relationship between Fiona and Paul might go, he gave the pastor the answer he wanted to hear. "I'm pretty sure she didn't," he said. "She's just moody at the minute."

"That's a relief," said Paul, getting up and shaking Carlos's hand with enthusiasm. "Please catch these people, Carlos."

"Don't worry. The net's closing in on them," said Carlos. "We'll catch them. If you hear anything else, ring me. The fact that these guys met today might mean they're planning something tonight. Anything you tell me will be in confidence. But don't, whatever you do, try to track Nicolae down or ask questions about him. I really don't want to find you dead inside this building."

"I'm not afraid of dying, but I feel I've got a lot more work to do before my time comes, so I'll heed your advice."

"One more thing," said Carlos.

"What?"

"Be wary of Ruby; after our conversation with Princess, we think she might work for Nicolae."

Paul paled again. "I appreciate the warning."

24

Castle Gardens bloomed with late-flowering shrubs as Sara took Lady for a long walk. Autumnal leaves provided an array of colours, whilst the manicured lawns added the green contrast. The outing appeared therapeutic for Lady, not happy at being parted from her master but enjoying the peaceful green space as she ran back and forth, nose in the air. The pair shook off their recent trauma. This was just what the doctor – or vet in Lady's case – ordered. Taking care of Lady gave Sara a feeling of being useful again, and DI Cook's offer of a job needed mulling over. Hanging around Suki's flat while her friend went out to work just wasn't Sara's style. Usually an active person, moping around all day didn't suit her at all and made her feel low. Carlos had provided her with the opportunity to escape from a state of inertia, and looking after Lady came easily.

Grey clouds appeared overhead, threatening rain, and the air chilled quickly as the sun disappeared. "Okay, Lady, I think we've walked for long enough. I'm not sure how Suki will feel about having a dog in her flat, so let's go back to your office, shall we?"

Lady cocked her head to one side as though listening and gave what Sara interpreted to be an affirmative whine. Carlos had given Sara a key because his PA had a day off. He also suggested she use the front door so that Lady wouldn't be nervous about going around the back without him. She wondered if Carlos thought the men who attacked him might return, but she doubted they would, at least not during the day.

With Lady on the lead, they passed the Jewry Wall Museum, and Sara glanced across the road to the Holiday Inn where she and Gary had eaten on Saturday night. They crossed the busy road, Lady behaving perfectly on the lead, and continued on to the high street. Traffic noises subsided when they arrived at the pedestrian-only route leading to the clock tower. Carlos's office was on the left. Impressed by how Lady sat while she unlocked the door to Carlos's front office, Sara noticed Lady's hackles rise accompanied by a warning growl.

Sara placed a hand on the dog's head as she moved away from the door.

"Let's just step aside for a minute," she said. Lady continued her low growling while Sara listened. Men's voices came from inside along with banging and clattering. She looked around, but nobody was within calling distance, so she pulled her phone from her pocket. Before she could dial 999, she felt a hand on her shoulder. Sara spun around to defend herself, her heart pounding, only to see Gary. His patrol car was parked across the road. Why hadn't she noticed it when they arrived?

"What's the matter?" he asked.

"Carlos asked me to look after his dog. We're just back from a walk and there's a burglary in progress."

"Stay there," Gary said. "I'll nip around the back and see what's going on."

"Call it in first," Sara shouted after him. No way could she confront burglars while Lady was with her; the poor animal had suffered enough.

"I will. Don't move, Sara." Gary disappeared, taking the side alley to the car park at the back. Lady continued growling, low and threatening. "It's okay, Lady? Gary's a friend; you met him the other night. Help will be here any minute. I will not let anyone hurt you." Lady's growling didn't let up when Gary came back. In fact, she snarled at him, baring her teeth.

"What did you see?" Sara asked.

"Not a lot. Help's on the way." Gary stared uncertainly at Lady, whose growling got louder. Sara reached down to reassure her.

"It's okay, Lady."

"What's the matter with her?" Gary asked.

"The trauma of the other night has made her neurotic," said Sara. "Carlos told me she's not been herself, which is why he didn't want to leave her on her own."

Gary kept a wary eye on Lady, saying. "Why don't you take her to your friend's? I'll stay and wait for backup."

"I'd rather see these people arrested for what they did to Carlos. I bet it's the same people. I'll call him."

"You don't need to do that now. Get away from here, Sara. Think of the dog."

There was a tension in Gary's voice Sara had never heard before. Lady was straining at the lead, standing in front of her as if to protect her. "Calm down, Lady," Sara said.

"It sounds like they're leaving out the back," Gary lowered his voice.

"Let's go inside then. We can hide until they drive out. I take it you got their registration number?" Sara opened the door, which she'd already unlocked. "I need to get Lady inside so they don't see her." Once inside and seeing nobody there, Sara removed Lady's lead, taking in the mess. Papers had been scattered across the floor, and Carlos's computer had disappeared. It was difficult to compute with Lady so unsettled. Her growling continued.

Gary tugged Sara's arm. "Look, I'm not happy being indoors with an angry dog; we should go out front and wait for backup."

"You wait out front while I go out the back and make sure they've gone." Sara started down the corridor leading to the back door.

"Don't, Sara."

Sara saw fear in Gary's eyes, the same look she'd seen the other night. The same suspicion crossed her mind that she'd wanted to tell Fiona about this morning, but she didn't want to believe her partner was a threat. She backed off as Gary moved nearer.

"It's okay, Sara, it's me."

Sensing danger, Sara sidestepped him and ran towards the front door, pulling it open.

"Get out, Lady."

Lady shot past her, running into the High Street, barking angrily. Nobody paid any attention apart from a woman pushing a pram, who hurried away as fast as she could in case there was a wild dog on the loose. Sara tried to follow her, but Gary was already pulling her back inside. Then she felt more arms grabbing her. Two men wearing balaclavas held her in a vice-like grip. She glared at Gary. "You're my partner. I trusted you!" She fought to get free, but they were too strong for her.

"Why didn't you just listen to me and go home?" said Gary, his eyes desperate. "Why do you always have to play the hero? What's the matter with you?"

"I'm a cop, Gary, and so are you."

"We'll take it from here," one of the men barked at Gary.

"That's unnecessary," said Gary, "she won't talk."

"Of course, she'll talk, and now she knows you're dirty. Do you really want to take that risk?"

"This isn't part of the deal."

"It's a bit late to think about your conscience now, mate," said one of the guys, pushing Gary away.

"You didn't call it in, did you?" Sara snapped. "Do it now, Gary, while you still can."

She felt her arm being twisted behind her back and pain shooting through her shoulder. It brought tears to her eyes, but she wouldn't cry.

"Save it, duck, he's been on the payroll a long time. He's got too much to lose, haven't you, PC Hodge?"

Sara looked from Gary to the man speaking. She wrestled

her left arm free from the one behind her, reached up and pulled the balaclava from the guy's face.

"You stupid..." the man cursed. Sara knew what to do next; she turned around and slapped Gary's face, scratching it. When the first man pinned her hands and tethered them in front of her with a cable tie, the other shouted. "Get that firebrand out of here. You go back to work, PC Hodge." The derision in his voice was clear. "There's nothing here."

"What about the dog?" asked the man holding Sara.

"Leave it. We can't go chasing a dog along the High Street, and in broad daylight there's CCTV everywhere. Hodge might catch it."

"No way," Gary said. "That dog's unpredictable and dangerous."

"Let's hope she doesn't get to you before I do, Gary," Sara yelled, sounding braver than she felt.

"Let's get out of here," the man holding Sara steered her towards the back door. "She's stronger than she looks." As Sara was forced through the back door, she realised the man without the balaclava was the man with a limp she had seen at Foxdale Church. They bundled her into the boot of a Mercedes, adding another cable tie to her ankles and a gag around her mouth before closing her in. While bouncing around as they left the car park, Sara heard Lady barking.

"Don't chase. Run, girl, run for your life," she thought, happy that Lady's fear had kept her from trying to attack Gary.

It took a while for the desperation to settle and Sara's heart to slow down; her eyes adjusted to the lack of light and she realised the men had been in too much of a hurry to think about her phone. Thanking God that the men had bound her hands in front rather than behind, she set about trying to get the phone from her pocket. Rolling onto her side and wedging herself in position for long enough, she retrieved it.

She dropped it a few times before holding it steadily in her left hand. It took a torturous amount of time, but eventually she managed to type a text.

25

Carlos left Foxdale Baptist and saw Fiona and Barry were about to climb into DC Barry King's patrol car. He quickened his pace. "Hold up, Fiona."

Fiona paused but was looking over his shoulder, scowling. Carlos turned to see Paul standing at the door, but not attempting to approach. Carlos walked as fast as he could while gripping his ribs. "Thanks for making it easy on me," he said sarcastically. "You don't deserve me, you know that?"

"Sorry. I forgot about your ribs. What did he have to say?" Fiona still sounded bitter, but he recognised her emotional pain.

"I'll explain later, but trust me, Paul's not involved."

"Thank God for that," Fiona's eyes shone a little as she gave Paul a wave before turning back to the patrol car. "I'd better get on or I'll be late."

Carlos's phone pinged, and he checked the text that had come through. "Oh, no!" he shouted.

Fiona stopped again, her forehead creased. "What is it?"

"Read this."

As Fiona read the text message, Carlos's head was spinning.

'Carlos, Gary's involved. They've got me in the boot of a grey Mercedes. Lady got away; she's somewhere on High Street. She chased for a while, but I hope she'll go back to your office as soon as the coast's clear. They wrecked your office. Hurry! One of the men works for Michael Kingsland; I saw his face. We've been driving for about twenty-five minutes. Ask Fiona to track this phone, find Lady, and pick up Gary.'

Fiona's eyes were wide when she finished reading. "Shoot! Change of plans."

"Is something wrong?" Paul was at Fiona's side, concern filling his face. He looked as though he were about to pull her into a hug, but she moved away.

"We'll talk later," she said. "Carlos, forward me that number."

Carlos did as asked.

Fiona handed Barry her phone and ran around to the driver's side. "Barry, I need a track on this number. Right, all in!"

Carlos climbed in the back while Barry had no choice but to jump in the passenger seat and pick up the radio.

Fiona looked at Barry as she started the engine. "PC Sara Ransom's been kidnapped. We need the route that phone's taking ASAP. While you're at it, put a call out to arrest PC Gary Hodge and ask uniform to pick up Carlos's dog, a springer spaniel called Lady, from Leicester High Street."

"Cancel that last one," Carlos said, still trying to fasten his seatbelt as Fiona screeched out of Foxdale towards the city centre. "I'll phone Julie. Lady won't trust many people at the moment. I'm sure Julie will have finished shopping by now."

"Okay, forget about the dog, but do the rest urgently and send someone to investigate a break-in at Jacobi Private Investigator's office on the High Street."

Barry relayed the message coherently, and the controller replied. "Got it, Ma'am."

Carlos appreciated not having to be the driver in a high-speed car chase because his rib pain was back with a vengeance. As soon as he was fastened in, he called Julie on speakerphone. She answered immediately.

"Julie, I can't go into details now, but the office has been broken into and Lady's loose on the High Street. Police are aware of the robbery, but finding Lady is a priority."

"Don't worry, Carlos, I'll find her. She'll be safe with me. You do what you've got to do." Carlos thanked God that he had a dependable and practical PA.

Fiona headed towards High Street. "I don't know where we're going yet, but I've got a pretty good idea it'll be a place owned by Michael Kingsland. He's in this up to his eyes."

"Paul told me one of Kingsland's guys was at the meeting in the church this morning. It was definitely one of the men who attacked me, and I'm sure Kingsland's man set fire to your boat. Paul identified one of the men meeting in his annexe this morning as one of Kingsland's protection detail. The guy had a limp." Carlos caught Fiona's eye in the rearview mirror. "Is there anything to drink in here?"

"What's up? Didn't Paul make you a drink?"

Carlos held his side. "If we're going to do this, I need to take some painkillers."

Fiona looked at Barry. "Sorry, no."

"Fair enough." Fiona held the steering wheel with one hand while reaching inside a raincoat pocket. "Here, take this."

Barry took the can of lemonade from Fiona and handed it to Carlos.

Carlos took two ibuprofen and two paracetamol, swigging them down with the lemonade. "Let's hope I can still fight if it comes to it, although at this rate, your guys will get there before us."

"It's difficult to drive fast when I don't know where I'm going, Carlos. What's keeping them with the trace?"

"Michael Kingsland's friends in high places will not stop him going down," Carlos said, a grim determination on his face. "I just hope they don't hurt Sara."

"We could do with more evidence against him," Fiona said. "Barry, get onto control and ask why they haven't got that trace yet."

Barry pressed the buttons on the radio and got through to despatch. "It's DC King, I'm with DI Cook in pursuit of a Mercedes, we need to know where to go."

"Just sending you the location now. They are driving on the B6047 heading south, Ma'am."

"On our way," Barry replied.

"Tell them to send backup to meet us there," Fiona yelled as she turned the siren on and took a sharp right turn.

"Already on their way, Ma'am."

"Have they found Hodge yet?" Fiona asked.

"We'll let you know as soon as they have him, Ma'am. His patrol car's on High Street, but there's no sign of him."

Barry kept the channel open while Fiona concentrated on driving.

Carlos's phone pinged with a text. "Is that Sara?" Fiona asked.

"No. Julie's found Lady. She's fine apart from being anxious."

"At least that's one positive," Fiona said, keeping her eye on the road as she sped past cars pulling out of the way. Every so often she had to slow down when they hit heavy traffic to give cars time to move, but they were soon heading out of the city and into open countryside.

Carlos replied to the text, asking Julie to take Lady to her house before concentrating on the road. "They are going to have to turn off before too long."

"There's farmland past Shangton," Barry said, bringing up a map of where they were headed on the dashboard.

Carlos felt a knot in his stomach as Fiona sped along the B road. They passed hedgerows and fields before the rain started again. Fiona had to slow down to meet the conditions.

"They'd better not hurt my new DC," Fiona was trying to keep it light-hearted, but they all knew these men couldn't let her go.

"We have to get to her before they do," Carlos said.

"I know," Fiona glanced briefly in the rearview. "These guys have no conscience. Look, we're getting closer so I need to switch the siren and the lights off."

"Speed up." Carlos was feeling agitated.

"It's tricky; I can't risk them doing something stupid if they see us."

"Yes, but they're getting away." Carlos's voice sounded as tense as he felt. He wished the pain in his ribs would settle, or he was going to have to conquer severe pain. His army training would help with that if it came to it. At least Barry was with them.

"They're turning off." Fiona yelled into the radio. "How far out is backup?"

"Five minutes," the dispatcher replied.

Fiona slowed down after five hundred yards and turned left. The men had turned onto a dirt track, which they followed for a mile and a half. To the left, a closed gate stood in their way.

"They're not taking any chances," Fiona said.

"Leave the car here," Carlos said. "We don't want them to hear us coming."

Fiona parked the car and got on the radio again. "I need those patrol cars. Tell them to move it. We're going in on foot."

"Yes, Ma'am."

The trio climbed over the gate rather than wasting time opening and closing it. There was a gap in the hedge that provided camouflage. Two fields ran parallel to the gravel track. "We need to hurry," said Carlos.

"Barry, you take the left field to that outhouse over there. We'll follow this one."

Barry did as ordered while Carlos tried to pick up speed.

"I don't think you should jog, Carlos. You'll be in agony."

Gritting his teeth and hoping he wouldn't do himself too much damage, he ignored her and set off slowly. Fiona was running, but her fitness levels, even without pain, weren't up to running through a field in the pouring rain. He looked behind.

"Don't worry about keeping up," he called, "do what you can."

"I'll be right behind you." Fiona doubled over as she waved him ahead.

With the endorphins kicking in and helping to control his pain, Carlos grabbed his right side and increased his pace. Any other time this would be easy, but with every breath making his ribs feel as if they might break. This was as bad as any assault course he'd faced in his past. After jogging half a mile, he was relieved to stop. The grey Mercedes was parked in front of a barn; Carlos shot a text to Fiona to call Barry back. There was just one car, and Carlos hoped Sara was right about there only being two men. He crept across the yard, watching where he trod, until he got to the car. Quietly, he opened the boot. It was empty. No surprise there. Carlos clicked it shut and crept around, using the car to stay out of sight. With his pain now moderate rather than severe, he tiptoed to the entrance of the large barn.

He could see Sara lying on her side on the straw-filled ground. She must have been terrified and in pain but wasn't giving the men the satisfaction of whimpering.

The two men stood a few feet away from Carlos, having a whispered argument.

"I don't want to do it." Neither man had balaclavas over their heads now. Carlos grinned when he noticed the one limping. At least he wouldn't be as hard to take out of the equation. Carlos looked behind him and saw Fiona about fifty yards away. He waved for her to keep the noise down.

"You ring him," the bigger guy told the one with the limp.

Reluctantly, the man made the call. "We have a problem. While we were at the private detective's office, an off-duty cop got in our way. She snatched Bob's balaclava and scratched Hodge's face when he helped us catch her. We've got her at the barn."

Carlos could hear a raised voice coming from the other end of the call but couldn't make out the words.

"Sorry, we didn't know what else to do. What do you want us to do with her? Okay. Got it."

"Well, what did he say?" the big guy named Bob asked.

"He said to torch the barn. She'll have yours and Hodge's DNA on her."

"Should I knock her out first?"

Sara was struggling with all her might to wrestle free of the ties, but was getting nowhere, just like Carlos a few nights before.

"No. Let's get out of here. We don't want to leave any evidence; burn her alive."

Sara tried to shout through the gag. Bob bent over her. "Ah, don't you want to die, duck? You should have thought of that before you removed my balaclava and scratched your partner – or – ex-partner's face."

Carlos took advantage of the situation while Limpalong

was distracted preparing to set the barn on fire. He crept up behind Bob, who was still leaning over Sara, kicking him in the side with all his strength. The man rolled away while the limping guy tried to run at Carlos. Carlos sidestepped and used an elbow to knock him to the ground. He already had his army knife out and cut Sara's ties as Bob recovered and ran towards him.

"Get out of here, Sara," Carlos yelled while dodging the moron. They toppled onto a bale of hay; Bob grabbed a pitchfork.

The guy with the limp tried to chase Sara, but Fiona stood in his way, pointing a taser. He decided surrender might be a better option, but Bob would not give in so easily. He lunged at Carlos with the pitchfork while Carlos struggled to dodge back and forth, his ribs screaming in pain.

"This time you're going to die, Jacobi."

"No. This time you're going to be arrested," said Carlos. Giving Fiona a nod. Barry cuffed limp-guy and Fiona fired the taser. Bob fell to the floor, and once he was down, Fiona used her cuffs to pin his wrists behind his back.

When Fiona and Carlos forced Bob to his feet, he looked dazed. "You're under arrest," she said, reading him his rights.

Two patrol cars with flashing blue lights arrived, and four officers stepped out, taking control of the prisoners.

"Hang on a minute." Carlos said, looking at the guy with the limp. "Give me your phone... Oh, sorry, you can't reach it. Don't worry, I'll get it for you." Carlos reached into the man's jeans pocket and took out the phone. "Look at the last number," he said.

"Get a trace on this number," Fiona said to one of the officers, who took it to his car.

Minutes later, the man was back. "The number belongs to Michael Kingsland."

Fiona spoke to the man with the limp. "What's your name?"

"Wally," Fiona tried to hide a smirk. "Right Wally. Call Michael and put the phone on speaker. Tell him you've done what he asked."

"Why should I?" he asked.

"Because if you do, I'll mention to the CPS how you cooperated. If you don't... well." She shrugged her shoulders. "You're looking at doing time either way, but it might help a lawyer plead your case."

Wally hit the dial button with the phone on speaker.

"Is it done?" Carlos recognised Michael Kingsland's voice immediately.

"Yep. All done, we're just waiting for it to catch."

"Is the officer inside?"

"Yes sir. The girl's in there. Before she's burned alive, I just want to make sure you want us to do this?"

"Of course I'm sure. You said she'd seen Bob. Get it done. Damn waste of a good barn."

"It's done, sir." He hung up.

"We all heard that. Take these two in while Barry takes us to retrieve Jacobi's car. Then we'll pay Mr Kingsland a visit."

"Yes, Ma'am."

"Are you all right, Sara?" Fiona asked.

"I will be when these men are charged along with my

former partner." Sara sounded exhausted, but her jaw was set with a determination Carlos admired.

"Well done, Sara," Carlos said. "Sending the text was quick thinking. And thanks for saving Lady again."

"I'm just glad these idiots didn't take my phone," Sara said, glaring at Bob, who had mocked her. She marched over to him. "Never call a woman, duck."

Fiona grinned, turning to one of the officers. "Take Sara with you and get a statement from her. Make sure she's checked over by a medic and take good care of her."

"Yes, Ma'am." Sara took a seat in the back of the second vehicle while the men were put in the back of a van.

"This time you lead," Carlos said to Fiona as they walked back to Barry King's car, which had been moved onto a grass verge.

"I'll call the super on the way." Fiona threw the keys back to Barry. "Use the blue lights because I'm seriously low on blood sugar."

"Good to see you've got your priorities right, DI Cook," Carlos said with a grin.

"Sorry, Ma'am, not allowed to use the lights for food," Barry said.

"You're a good detective, Barry. Just get me there within the law, ASAP."

26

On the way back to Foxdale Baptist Church, Fiona informed her superintendent of what had transpired and the arrests made so far. She also explained the conversation they had overheard between Kingsland and Wally Tyrell. Superintendent Henley was brief and to the point, highlighting that any evidence obtained must be solid. Fiona assured her that numerous officers had heard and Carlos had recorded a telephone call between Wally Tyrell and Michael Kingsland. "The former willingly gave his boss up, Ma'am. I'm certain he'll testify."

"Make the arrest then, Fiona, but keep it low profile, don't go in with flashing lights and patrol cars."

"We'll be sure to keep it off the radar, Ma'am. We don't want Nicolae warned again," she said.

It was nearing 5 p.m. when Barry dropped them off.

When they walked inside the church, Paul was waiting for them. "Through to the annexe, please," he said, beaming a welcome. "I was told these were for a DI Cook." He held two large takeaway bags in his hands. "Either you've got an enormous appetite, or you're expecting guests."

Fiona grinned. "I thought you might like to join us while we explain where we've got to. Carlos thought you'd be pleased to hear we arrested two of the guys meeting here this morning."

Paul's eyes shone even brighter. Carlos suspected it had as much to do with being back in Fiona's good books as the information about their arrests. "In that case, I'd be delighted. Come inside."

"I'm afraid we'll need to be quick. Carlos and I still have work to do, but if I don't eat, I'm likely to kill the guy we're about to arrest."

"We can't have that. I'll get the plates," said Paul, placing the bags on the table.

"You two make a start; I just want to ring Julie and ask how Lady is." Carlos wanted to check on Lady, but he also wanted to give Fiona and Paul time to make up. When he headed back into the annexe, laughter greeted him. It was good to hear Fiona laughing again.

Fiona pushed a plate toward him. "Help yourself, Carlos, and take your time. It appears Michael is on his way to an investment meeting in Coventry and much as I'd like to arrest him in full view of his investors, I'm under orders to keep it low-profile. I've just got off the phone with the super, and she says we can make the arrest first thing tomorrow. I've got DC Maplin tailing him to make sure he doesn't disappear, but I doubt he'll try to contact his goons again tonight."

Carlos would rather have got on with the arrest, but he

was as keen as Fiona not to give Nicolae any clues that the net was closing in.

"Anything on PC Hodge?" he asked, helping himself to a chicken biryani. Fiona had ordered five different dishes, leaving plenty of choice. He also picked up a naan bread.

"They've got him in a holding cell. I'll interview him with Hugh after you drop me off at the station."

"Your taxi awaits, Ma'am," he said with a chuckle.

~

The next morning Fiona arrived at Carlos's office early, throwing her handbag on the table while making herself a coffee.

"I take it you didn't have a good night either?" Carlos asked.

"Hodge isn't talking. In fact, he denied everything, even when I told him we caught Sara's abductors. He's trying to say it's Sara who has been in league with them. In the end, we left him to stew. He'll realise it's pointless once we get CCTV from the High Street."

"I already heard Bob implicate him when they were in the barn."

"Good. That's extra pressure we can apply, but right now I can't wait to get to Kingsland. DC Maplin says he stayed the night in Coventry but left first thing this morning. He's in his office. I'd rather have arrested him at home, but I don't want to wait any longer. We'll just have to make it as low-key as possible."

Half an hour later, Carlos pulled up outside Kingsland

Enterprises, and he and Fiona entered the building. They bypassed the main reception and took the lift to the fourth floor. Once in the right place, Fiona ignored Priscilla's protestations and marched straight through to Michael Kingsland's office with the receptionist hot on their heels.

As Fiona entered, Priscilla ran ahead. "I'm sorry, Mr Kingsland, they barged past me."

Kingsland's face darkened. Less than twenty-four hours ago, he'd ordered his men to murder a police officer. He had to be wondering whether their arrival had something to do with that.

"What is it now, Inspector? I'm busy."

Fiona crossed the room gleefully. Carlos was pleased she'd eaten, or Kingsland might have made for good eating.

"Michael Kingsland. I'm arresting you on conspiracy to commit murder, conspiracy to engage in actual bodily harm against Mr Carlos Jacobi, conspiracy to commit arson, and animal cruelty. I expect further charges will follow. You do not have to say anything, but it may harm your defence if you do not mention when questioned something which you later rely on in court. Anything you do say may be given in evidence. Do you understand?"

Priscilla stopped complaining. Instead, she stared open-mouthed at her boss.

Kingsland glared at Carlos and Fiona, and then at his PA.

"Don't just stand there, Priscilla, call my lawyer. I don't know what this is all about, Inspector. But I can assure you I'll be free within half an hour."

"Not this time, Mr Kingsland. You see, Mr Jacobi and I, along with several officers, were with Mr Tyrell when he called you yesterday. We heard him ask if you really wanted him to set fire to a barn in order to kill a serving police officer."

Kingsland's sweaty brow suggested Fiona had got to him, but he wouldn't go down without a fight. "That's nonsense; you must have misheard."

"In which case, you'll be pleased to hear that the officer is alive and well and able to give evidence of everything she heard your men say. We also believe you conspired to murder at least one other, who did, sadly, die."

"Who?"

"Mrs Jodie Whitwick."

"I did not."

"We know your men have links to Tyson Jerome, who orchestrates riots. The riots provided cover for the murders of three women. Including your sworn enemy, Jodie Whitwick."

"You're making a huge mistake, DI Cook, you can't pin any of this on me."

"Your men met with Tyson Jerome regularly. Jerome orchestrated the riots for which we hold you responsible. Unless, of course, you want to correct us and give us another name."

"I'm not saying another word until I've seen my lawyer."

"Fair enough," said Fiona. "Let's go down to the station. As a courtesy, Mr Kingsland, we will not handcuff you but ask you not to resist arrest and come with us."

With a heavy sigh, Kingsland nodded. They passed Priscilla's desk on the way out.

Carlos had a quick word. "We would prefer to keep your

boss's name out of the news for now. Can we count on your silence?"

The loyal PA glared at him, nodding. "You're wrong about Mr Kingsland," she said defiantly.

An hour later, Carlos watched Fiona and DS Hugh Barber interview Michael Kingsland. Kingsland and his lawyer had spoken for thirty minutes alone to discuss matters before the interview.

From the moment Fiona entered the room, she followed the procedure of switching on the tape, stating who was present at the interview, informing them that the interview was being recorded.

"I'd like to make it clear," Kingsland's lawyer stated. "My client will cooperate with your inquiries."

"Good," Fiona said. "Mr Kingsland, can you tell us who orchestrated the riots on the nights each woman's body was found?"

Kingsland took a hard swallow before replying. "A man named Nicolae Romanescu."

Finally, someone willing to give Nicolae up to save his own skin. Carlos couldn't be happier.

"And who was responsible for the murders of Angela Morris, Diane Foster and Jodie Whitwick?"

"Nicolae Romanescu."

"Are you just making accusations to clear your name, or do you have evidence?"

Kingsland checked with his lawyer, who nodded.

"I have evidence. I recorded every interview, every conversation."

"And you realise the recordings will incriminate you?" Fiona asked.

Kingsland once more checked with his lawyer and received the same response.

"Yes."

"Where can we find Mr Romanescu?" Fiona was playing it cool, but Carlos knew just how excited she would be under the surface. He was impressed.

"He's difficult to find, but I have an address he uses for his respectable persona. He owns a mansion in the suburbs. It's registered under a different name, Novak Reisling. Nicolae has multiple aliases, but that's his favourite. He's also a master of disguise. Don't be taken in by the cream suit identification method. He only wears that to throw people off his scent."

Everything was falling into place. Carlos felt tension in his shoulders but also relaxed, if the two feelings were possible simultaneously. The tension wouldn't disappear until Nicolae was arrested and all the evidence they compiled against him was used to lock him away for a very long time.

"I understand Mr Romanescu is involved in other criminal activities. Could you tell us anything about those?" Fiona asked.

Kingsland was happy to shift the blame away from himself. "You name it, he's got a finger in it. Modern slavery, drugs, smuggling, and the illegal sex trade."

"How do we know this is his business and not yours?" Fiona was fishing for evidence.

"As well as the recordings, we had an arrangement for

him to use some of my buildings. I didn't know what he was doing at first, and by the time I did..."

"Don't tell me," Fiona said, "he had something on you."

"Something like that," said Kingsland.

The lawyer intervened. "My client is cooperating fully; I expect this to be considered at trial, Detective Inspector."

"I'm sure he'll be able to do a deal with the CPS," said Fiona. "I just want to catch Nicolae Romanescu and close his operation once and for all. If your client can help with this, we'd all appreciate it."

"Councillor Jodie Whitwick had evidence against him. He asked me to get hold of it."

"And did you?"

Kingsland nodded. "I told him I destroyed it, but I didn't trust him, so I kept it."

Carlos felt his heart skip a beat. At last they had him, but something bothered him. He texted Fiona, who read the text and asked.

"One thing I'm not clear about, Mr Kingsland. Can you tell me why Nicolae used your men to orchestrate the riots?"

"They're not my men," Kingsland spat the words out. "Not really. They're paid to do my bidding, but Nicolae pays them, and I'm pretty sure their loyalty lies with him."

Fiona shifted in her chair, clenching and unclenching her fists at her side before asking. "Which one of you ordered your men to attack PI Carlos Jacobi and torch my boat?"

Kingsland shook his head vigorously. "That was Nicolae, but the men went beyond what he ordered, which he wasn't happy about. To be honest, I would have fired them long before now, but it suits him to keep them working with me. I spoke to Nicolae when Gary Hodge told me what had happened."

Fiona sat upright. "Does Gary work for you or for Nicolae?"

"For me. He keeps me informed of what goes on, and I pay him for doing so."

"Why was he at Jacobi's office when the men broke in yesterday?"

"Since the events of Saturday night, I've asked him to let me know if they do anything else stupid. He called me after they took your officer yesterday." Kingsland put his head in his hands. "If she hadn't ripped Bob's balaclava off and if she hadn't known about Gary, she would have been released."

Fiona shook her head. "You ordered those men to kill a police officer. That won't be overlooked no matter what the circumstances," Fiona said.

After a few follow-up questions, Fiona concluded the interview.

27

Fiona had put everything into today's planned operation. Every waking hour for weeks had been spent poring over statements, timelines, surveillance logs and legal authorisations. She had coordinated officers across the serious crime team, liaised with regional units, and sat through more briefings than she cared to count. It was the biggest operation of her life.

While DCI Malcolm Flatley and Superintendent Henley were officially in overall charge, they had made it clear from the outset that Fiona would take the lead wherever possible. Flatley's calm, understated authority and Henley's strategic oversight provided a reassuring backdrop, but it was Fiona who had knitted the disparate strands together. She was grateful and proud of the confidence they placed in her.

"Don't get used to it," Flatley had said during one of the initial briefings, a smile creasing his mouth. "I'll be reclaiming my authority once this is over."

"I'd expect nothing less, sir," Fiona had replied.

The raids had taken weeks to organise. Every premise Nicolae used had been identified, mapped, and risk assessed. Entry teams were assigned, timings shared, warrants checked and double-checked. There would be no room for error. If one site was taken too early because a team moved at the wrong time, the entire operation could unravel.

At the centre of it all was Michael Kingsland.

Fiona had kept Nicolae in the dark about the real reason for Kingsland's short arrest. As far as Kingsland's remaining protection detail was concerned, Kingsland had been arrested for a breach of planning law resulting in a gas explosion at one of his premises, during which three workers had been injured. Nicolae hadn't questioned it because the incident had happened, and Kingsland's corner-cutting was well known.

What Nicolae didn't know was that Fiona had used the incident when Kingsland confessed to the explosion that had happened six months prior to his arrest. He'd also confessed to a raft of other crimes. False accounting, bribery, exploitation. All this to cut a deal with the CPS, and he would give them Nicolae Romanescu in exchange.

Kingsland, true to his word, had supplied Fiona with evidence of money laundering payments from Nicolae: bank transfers through shell companies, coded ledger entries, and cash movements. More damning was the video evidence. Footage from discreetly placed cameras showed Nicolae visiting each premises at regular intervals.

Michael Kingsland must have spent years preparing himself for the day he'd be arrested by gathering mountains of evidence that would be used to charge Nicolae

Romanescu. Fiona could only assume he had always intended to have an insurance policy.

They released Michael Kingsland on bail to enable him to continue business as usual without Nicolae suspecting anything was amiss.

Kingsland had agreed to wear both a wire and a tag so they could keep tabs on him. He was much more interested in the deal he'd cut with the CPS than he was about betraying Nicolae, who he told Fiona he'd never liked.

Carlos and Fiona had little choice but to trust that Michael didn't give Nicolae any clue that his business was about to come crashing down around his head.

The new DC Sara Ransom volunteered to keep a close watch on Tyson Jerome, especially since returning home to her mother's. Sara told everyone except her mum she was no longer a police officer, and now she wore civilian clothing, they believed her. It meant Tyson barely gave her a second glance when their paths crossed.

At significant risk to herself, another young detective from north of the patch went undercover as an independent sex worker to befriend and observe Ruby. Neither suspected that their activities were being monitored. Paul introduced the young sex worker, Emerald, to Ruby and asked Ruby to look after her, as he worried she might need support. Paul also continued to tell Ruby that Fiona and Carlos were worried about Princess and that he hadn't been able to contact her.

Paul was turning out to be a reliable operative, although Fiona hated putting him in a compromised position.

"You tell me if it gets too much," she'd told him firmly.

He'd nodded. "I will, but I want to help."

Ruby checked in with Paul regularly, feigning concern about Princess, but it also meant Paul could ask about the fake Emerald and was given no indication that Ruby suspected anything was amiss. All Emerald's clients were fake, something they could keep up for a few weeks without alerting Ruby, who was more interested in keeping in with Paul to find out about Princess.

Ruby wasn't stupid enough to meet directly with Nicolae, but she was frequently seen with Tyson Jerome. Tyson met with lots of people, including drug pushers, violent thugs and Kingsland's remaining men, but never with Nicolae.

Tyson and the rest of Kingsland's detail believed Kingsland's two men under arrest were sunning themselves in the Caribbean. Kingsland had suggested to Nicolae that they take a holiday because Fiona and Carlos had been asking about them in particular.

The morning of the operation dawned grey and still. Fiona barely touched her breakfast. Her stomach churned with nerves and anticipation as she checked her equipment for the third time.

Carlos noticed. "You'll wear a hole in that radio if you keep fiddling with it."

She forced a smile. "Humour me."

They were parked outside Nicolae's mansion along with two patrol cars, engines idling. The house loomed large behind its wrought-iron gates, all pale stone and manicured hedges. It looked peaceful. Respectable.

"Appearances mean nothing," she muttered.

Carlos agreed.

DCI Flatley would lead the raid on the largest premises, the factory staffed by so-called modern slaves. Superintendent Henley was coordinating from control and would give the go-ahead.

Fiona checked her watch. One minute.

She met Carlos's gaze. "Ready?"

"Ready."

"Operation Nicolae is a go. I Repeat. Go."

On cue, two officers opened the mansion's gates. The car surged forward, blue lights flashing as they swept through and pulled up in front of Nicolae's home. Officers spilled out, taking up their positions, cameras following their every move.

Fiona stepped forward and rang the doorbell.

They waited.

Nothing.

She rang it again, longer this time. Still no reply.

She raised her voice. "Police! Open up."

Silence.

"Okay," she said evenly. "We're coming in."

She stepped back and gave a clear thumbs-up. The team with the battering ram moved into position. One sharp crack echoed through the morning air as the door gave way.

They flooded inside.

The house was immaculate, almost unnervingly so. But it appeared empty.

"Clear!" came the calls, one after another, as rooms were searched.

Then a shout came from the rear of the property. "Movement outside!"

Fiona ran, heart hammering, just in time to see the back gates swing open. A motorbike roared to life, tyres spitting gravel as it took off, taking the officers at the back of the building by surprise.

"Nicolae!" Carlos shouted.

They were back in the car in seconds, sirens wailing as they tore down the drive. Nicolae was fast, weaving through traffic with reckless confidence. Fiona kept him in sight as long as she could, relaying updates over the radio.

"He's heading north. High speed. Motorbike."

"Air support is en route," came the reply.

Nicolae veered suddenly, swerving off the road and into open land. The patrol car went as far as it could before the terrain defeated them.

The helicopter arrived a few minutes later, its rotor blades thumping overhead as it circled, but within minutes the inevitable was confirmed.

"Helicopter unable to find him, Ma'am."

Fiona closed her eyes, frustration washing over her.

They returned to the mansion in grim silence. Inside, the signs were obvious once you knew where to look. Filing cabinets stood open and empty. Shredded paper littered the floor. The safe in the study gaped wide, its contents gone.

"He knew," Carlos said quietly.

Fiona nodded, her jaw tight. "Someone tipped him off."

Around them, officers continued their searches, but the victory had soured. Nicolae Romanescu was gone.

Again.

Fiona stepped outside, drawing in a deep breath. The operation had been flawless in every respect. Arrests were being made across the city. Victims were being freed. Evidence seized.

But the man they wanted most had slipped through their fingers.

And that, Fiona knew, was a problem they would have to face next.

28

It had been three days since Nicolae's escape, with no sightings. All aliases and disguises had been passed on to port and airport authorities, and Fiona said the authorities were as sure as can be that Nicolae was still in the country.

A thought had come to Carlos in the night, not sure whether it was a dream or in a period of semi-wakefulness, but the idea registered as a good one, which he shared with Fiona.

He phoned Tony Hadden and waited for what seemed an eternity while the phone rang and rang. He waited so long that he could hear his own pulse in his ears like a syncopated thud. The anxiety of missing Nicolae lay heavy on his chest. Fiona watched him from across the interview room, her arms folded, one foot tapping a jittery rhythm on the floor.

"Come on, Tony," Carlos muttered, staring at the phone, willing Tony to pick up.

Eventually, he answered. Both Carlos and Fiona tensed as they heard the reporter's voice come through on the speaker.

"Carlos, are you trying to explode my phone? What can I do for you?" Tony's voice sounded more anxious than Carlos had ever heard before.

"Listen, Tony, I don't want to put you in any danger," he said, keeping his tone low and measured. "But I thought you'd like to know we're closing down Nicolae's operation. We raided all his premises and put a stop to his illegal activities. Our problem is. He got a tip-off and escaped when we raided his home. So far, he's slithered into hiding. I need to ask if you know where he might go?"

There was silence at the end of the phone for way too long while Tony considered. Carlos tried to remain patient. This wasn't the casual pause of someone working out what to say, but a loaded quiet of someone thinking about whether he would reply. Carlos could hear faint background noise – a TV on low. It felt miles away from the silence.

Carlos got to his feet, pacing the room with the phone on the table, forcing his jaw to unclench. The movement produced a dull ache in his ribs, but they were almost healed. Fiona arched an eyebrow. *Well?* Her expression asked.

He shrugged helplessly. "Tony?" Carlos prompted. "Are you still there?"

When Tony finally spoke, Carlos heard a tremor in his voice. "Are you sure you're going to get him, and that this will be the end for him?"

"We've got enough evidence to put him away for the rest of his life, but DI Cook and I need to find him. Tony, if you've got anything, anything at all?"

Another period of quiet, then Tony exhaled. "I can't tell you what a relief it would be. I've longed for his capture ever since that guy forced me off the road and almost killed me. I wanted to tell you about it when you phoned that night, but his men got inside."

Carlos stopped pacing and sat down at the table opposite Fiona. "Why didn't you say?"

"Because they would have got you as well," Tony snapped, then softened. "I had evidence I'd kept on an encrypted file on my computer. I tried to email it to you, but they were too quick for me and destroyed my PC. They bundled me into a car and told me to leave Leicester and never come back. I don't know what they did with my car."

"It's a shame about the destroyed evidence," Carlos said, "but we've got enough without it. If you have information that will help us track him down, I'd appreciate that more than anything. You know what he's like, and we're running out of time. The longer the trail stays cold; the more chance he has to come up with another identity and leave the country."

"If you're on to him, he'll do a runner like he did last time," Tony said flatly, "and then he'll get one of his corrupt cops to get rid of your evidence so he can come back again. If not, he'll set up his business in some other part of Europe."

"I understand," Carlos kept his tone level. He could feel Fiona's impatience burning the side of his face. "But let's not let him get away this time, Tony."

On the other end of the line, Tony hesitated again. Carlos heard the faint creak of floorboards and the scrape of a chair. When he spoke again, Tony sounded like a man pulling a knife out of his own stomach.

"He has a private jet he keeps in his own private airfield in Nottinghamshire. If he's not left already, it's under the name Nick Kristofferson."

Carlos straightened, adrenaline hitting his bloodstream. It was a name Kingsland had given them as one of Nicolae's aliases. Fiona's team was still poring through everything to do with all the names. Fiona's head snapped up, her eyes on his.

"Can you send me the address of the airport?" Carlos asked while nodding to Fiona.

"I'll text it," Tony said. "Along with the tail number. He won't fly commercial if he knows you'll be watching the airports, and he might try for a new identity."

Carlos heard the buzz a second later. Fiona stepped in closer, reading the message as it flashed up on his screen.

"Let me know if you get him, Carlos. I'd like to come home."

"I'd like that too," Carlos said.

He hung up immediately.

29

"Let's go," Fiona said, already moving. "I'll call air traffic control and check it's not gone anywhere."

"My guess is he's long gone," Carlos said, following her as she strode from the interview room to the incident room. She marched toward the operations desk.

"They still need permission to get in the air," she said, snatching up the landline. "And he must know we have his aliases. My guess is he's been salvaging as much money as he can before leaving the country and will hire another pilot. We'll make sure that plane stays grounded."

Fiona started with an initial call which ended with a fist pump. "It's not left yet. We have the fog to thank for that." It had been uncharacteristically foggy since Nicolae's escape, which matched Carlos's mood.

Fiona continued. "It's scheduled to leave tonight, so we need to hurry to get the authority in place." She got back on the phone, calling Superintendent Henley first. After ending that call, she made other calls barking orders down the line, identifying herself, requesting urgent authorisations, using words like *armed response* and *flight risk*. Carlos caught the keys she threw his way, his heart thumping an eager rhythm. Around them, the incident room snapped into a higher gear as chairs scraped back, radios clipped to uniforms, high-vis jackets were pulled on. The low murmur of officers suddenly turned sharp and purposeful.

By the time Fiona slammed the phone down, she had a grim smile on her face.

"The tower's been warned," she said. "They'll delay as long as they can. If he's already on site, he might try to jump ahead of the order. We need to move fast."

"What about Nottingham police?" Hugh Barber asked.

"Henley says no-one outside this room is to be involved because we still don't know who tipped him off last time. It's down to us and our armed response team."

"Then let's move," Carlos said.

"I need to stop off at the armoury," Fiona said.

Carlos had no idea that Fiona was firearms trained, but it might come in handy if the armed response team didn't get there fast enough. Once she had bulletproof vests for the two of them and a Glock 17 in her hands, they jogged along the corridor. The automatic doors at the station entrance slid open, and they burst into the chilled air.

They put the vests on while Fiona ran toward a marked BMW, its blue and yellow pattern dull under the grey sky. Fiona jumped into the driver's seat while Carlos sat in the passenger seat.

The satnav flickered on as Fiona tapped in the airfield coordinates Tony had sent.

"An hour in normal traffic," she muttered. "We need to do it in forty. I want to get there ahead of him."

Fiona hit the siren. The wail exploded into the street, making drivers ahead check their mirrors and move out of the way. They shot through the city, the patrol car carving a noisy path. Red lights became suggestions. She slowed just enough to be sure the junction was clear before roaring through. Carlos watched both the road and the screen; one hand braced on the dashboard.

"Left here," he said, pointing. "Take the ring road; it'll be faster than going through town."

She swung the car left, tyres squealing. The G-force shoved them both sideways, their shoulders thumping against the seat bolsters.

"Find out what's happening at the airfield," Carlos said.

She was already on the radio. "Control, this is DI Fiona Cook. En route to Notts private strip at..." she rattled off the coordinates "...in pursuit of high-risk target Nicolae Romanescu, alias Nick Kristofferson. Confirm if any units are on the scene. Over."

Static hissed, then a dispatcher came back, voice tight. "Be advised, armed response on the way, ETA twenty-five minutes. Airfield staff have acknowledged the ground order but report an aircraft already being prepared. No visual confirmation of suspect. Over."

"Tell armed response to stay outside the perimeter until we arrive," Fiona said. "No-one spooks him into the air and let me know if there's a sighting. Over."

"Copy that. Proceed with caution."

"Caution," Fiona muttered as she clipped the radio back. "Sure."

Fiona pushed the accelerator harder until they hit the M1. The sky seemed to drop lower; the clouds bruised purple along the horizon. A lorry drifted lazily into the right lane ahead of them, indicator flashing half-heartedly.

"For heaven's sake," Carlos breathed.

"I'll take the inside," Fiona said. "He'll be too slow to react."

She checked her mirrors, then dipped left, the siren screaming as they shot down the narrow strip of tarmac between the lorry and the hard shoulder. The gap shrank and his knuckles whitened on the wheel.

"Easy," Fiona muttered to herself.

Metal blurred inches from the car. Carlos held his breath as she nudged the wheel a fraction, and the BMW slipped past. They shot out into the outside lane again, the lorry's bulk sliding away behind them.

"Remind me never to criticise your parking again," Carlos said, exhaling. "Take the next exit," he commanded before the satnav had time.

The next road curved, the countryside rolling past in a smear of green and brown fields, trees rattling their autumnal leaves in the wind. The satnav pinged.

"Next exit, two miles," Carlos said. "We'll be on B-roads after that."

"Yep. I'll watch for tractors, suicidal dogs, the usual."

The rain started as a mist, then thickened quickly into a drizzle that streaked the windscreen. Carlos flicked on the wipers. Drops glittered in the strobes of their blue lights, turning the world into a jittery watercolour.

"Control," Fiona said into the radio again. "Any update from the airfield?"

"Tower reports jet engines spooling up," came the reply. "They're insisting no take-offs are allowed, but the pilot is protesting. No visual of the suspect boarding. Over."

"He's there," Carlos said. "And he knows we're coming. I hate to say this, Fiona, but there's a mole in your team." Carlos had thought that after Nicolae was able to escape through the back entrance when they raided his home. "He'll fly the plane himself if he has to."

Fiona cursed. "That' for another day. Right now, let's concentrate on the job in hand."

They took the exit. The road narrowed and was flanked by hedges so tall they were like green walls. The tarmac was rough but greasy with wet leaves; puddles lay in long, deceptive strips. Fiona eased off the accelerator a fraction. The patrol car still hurtled along; she silenced the siren and turned off the blue lights. One bad patch and they'd be upside down in a ditch while Nicolae took off overhead.

"Sharp right coming up," he warned, glancing between the satnav and the rain-smeared view ahead. "Ninety-degree turn. Try not to kill us."

The tyres shrieked as he threw the car into the corner. The back end twitched, briefly flirting with the idea of sliding out. Carlos braced, his hand shooting up to the grab handle. The BMW's wheels straightened, and it fired down the next stretch of road.

"See?" Fiona said, breathless. "Not dead."

"Yet," Carlos replied with a smile.

Five minutes of hard driving later, the landscape changed again. The hedgerows fell away, replaced by flat, open fields and, in the distance, a strip of tarmac cutting across the land like a grey scar. A low hangar squatted at its edges, and a chain-link fence ran along the perimeter, topped with spirals of barbed wire.

"There," Carlos said, pointing through the windscreen. "That's got to be it."

As they approached, the airfield's small control tower came into view, along with a white business jet, nose pointed toward the runway, its engine cowlings open and lights glowing along its fuselage.

The access road kinked left toward an unmanned security gate with a barrier arm.

"No time for polite," Fiona said, stamping on the brakes enough to shed speed, then she swerved, catching the barrier arm with the edge of the bull bar. It snapped up and over, splintering as it flew aside.

They were on the taxiway now; the runway stretched parallel to them. The jet's engines were turning, a heavy, throaty rumble that Carlos felt in his chest. The aircraft crept forward, its nose wheel turning toward the centreline. "He must already be on board," Carlos said.

Fiona aimed the patrol car along the access lane running beside the runway. The surface was smoother but slick with rain. She flicked the siren back on as they closed the distance.

"Control, this is DI Fiona Cook," Fiona said into the

radio, voice taut. "We have visual on the aircraft. Engines running, taxiing to the runway. We're on site. We're going to try to intercept before take-off. Over."

"Understood," came the reply. "Backup four minutes out."

"Four minutes might as well be four hours," Carlos muttered. "We need to stop that plane. How much trouble do we get for parking a patrol car in front of a private jet?" he asked, eyes fixed on the aircraft.

"Less than we'll get if we let him vanish into the clouds," Fiona said. "There's a crossroads just ahead. I'll floor it and cut across the nose before he lines up."

Carlos could see what she meant. A narrow service road bisected the runway, marked with yellow chevrons.

She dropped a gear and pressed the accelerator to the floor. The BMW lunged forward, the engine howling. The jet ahead angled onto the runway centre, its engines spooling louder, and picked up speed even as it taxied. Its lights glared through the rain.

"Come on, come on," Carlos hissed.

She spun the steering wheel, cutting sharply right. Tyres shrieked. For a moment, all Carlos could see was runway and rain and the blazing lights of the jet. Fiona slammed on the brakes.

The patrol car skidded to a stop sideways across the tarmac, blocking the jet's path. The nose of the aircraft loomed larger and larger, its engines roaring, the smell of kerosene thick even through the car's vents.

"Is he going to stop?" Fiona asked, her voice calm but cold.

Carlos stared at the oncoming aircraft, every muscle in his body tensed. If the pilot kept going, they'd all be pulp.

At the last possible moment, the jet's nose dipped. The engines throttled back with a deafening whine, and the aircraft shuddered as the brakes bit. Its nosewheel slewed slightly, tyres gripping wet tarmac, and it came to a halt barely ten feet in front of the patrol car.

The air between them shimmered with exhaust heat.

"Show-off," Carlos said.

Fiona exhaled shakily. "You're welcome."

They climbed out of the car, doors pushed open against the wash of hot, oily air. The rain fell harder now, drumming against the bonnet, soaking their hair and shoulders in seconds. Fiona drew her Glock 17 and held it low but ready.

"Armed police!" Fiona shouted, her voice cracking through the storm. "Shut down the engines and stay where you are!"

The jet's door remained closed. The engines stayed at idle, a stubborn, teeth-rattling growl.

"Control, this is DI Cook," Fiona said into her shoulder radio. "We have the aircraft stopped on the runway. No compliance yet. Request immediate armed backup on runway access. Over."

"Backup one minute out," came the reply. "Use extreme caution. Suspect may be armed."

"May," Carlos muttered. "That's cute."

The cockpit windows were a black mirror in the wet. After a moment, they saw a figure move inside. The engines spooled down; the roar easing off by increments. After a few long seconds, the whine dropped to a sullen hum.

"The door's our next problem," Fiona said.

The forward door finally cracked open with a hiss. The built-in staircase swung down in jerky increments, clanging as it locked into place.

A man in a pilot's uniform appeared at the top, hands already raised, eyes wide.

"Hands where I can see them!" Fiona shouted. "Step down slowly, one at a time!"

The pilot did as he was told, water slapping at his polished shoes as he descended. Carlos moved to meet him and cuffed him, while Fiona kept her focus on the dark rectangle of the cabin doorway.

"Anyone else on board?" Carlos barked at the pilot as he reached the tarmac.

"Just... just my passenger," the man stammered. "He said we had clearance, I swear—"

Carlos ordered. "Stay where you are. Don't move."

The pilot complied.

At the top of the stairs, a second figure appeared. Nicolae.

Even drenched in plane-cabin lighting and rain, he looked expensively composed. Dark coat, tailored. A neat, trimmed beard. A smile that never reached his eyes. He paused on the threshold, hands resting lightly on the door-frame, surveying the scene as if he were stepping out of a restaurant.

"Detective Inspector Cook," he called down, voice smooth. "And Mr Jacobi. What a surprise."

"Step down, Nicolae," Fiona said, her gun unwavering. "Slowly. Hands where I can see them."

He lifted his hands slightly, rain gleaming on his skin. "You know I'm a legitimate businessman."

"Legitimate businessmen don't need fake names for private jets," Carlos said. "Or warehouses full of trafficked girls."

Nicolae's eyes flickered, just for a moment, before his smile snapped back into place. He took one step down the stairs. Then another.

Carlos felt it more than saw it – the shift in weight, the subtle lowering of Nicolae's shoulder, the way his right hand dipped a fraction too far toward his coat. Training and instinct collided in his head.

"Gun!" he shouted.

Nicolae's hand flashed toward his hip. There was a metallic glint. Fiona moved first. Her shot cracked the air, the sound echoing off the tarmac.

Nicolae jerked, his body twisting as the bullet ripped through the meat of his shoulder. He tumbled sideways, missed a step, and crashed down the last few stairs, hitting the wet runway with a sickening thud.

For a second he lay there, stunned. The gun spun out of his hand and fell into the shadow under the plane's fuselage.

"Don't move!" Fiona yelled, advancing, her shoes splashing through standing water.

Nicolae groaned, his free hand clutching at his bleeding shoulder. Blood slicked his fingers, mixing with the rain in thin pink rivulets.

Carlos swept past him, kicking the fallen gun further away, sending it spinning into the dark.

Blue lights approached from the far end of the runway as

backup units flooded through the broken barrier, vehicles fanned in a semicircle. Officers spilled out, weapons drawn, voices shouting commands that overlapped and tangled in the rainy air.

Carlos dropped to one knee beside Nicolae, pressing his own hand down hard over the wound, both to stem the blood and to keep him pinned.

"You're not dying today," Carlos said, breath fogging in the cold air. "You don't get off that easy."

Nicolae grimaced, teeth bared. "You think this changes anything?" he hissed. "You won't keep me forever."

Fiona loomed over them, rain plastering her hair to her face, gun still pointed down. The fury in her eyes was icy, controlled.

"We don't need forever," she said. "We just need long enough for a jury to hear what you've done."

She nodded to Hugh Barber, who came off his radio after requesting an ambulance. "Cuff him. Let the medic treat that shoulder and then get him in a van. Hugh, watch him every second. We can't afford to lose him again."

"Don't worry, I've got this," Hugh said, "glad to see you're both alive."

As the armed response team surged forward, taking over, Carlos rose slowly, his legs tingling from the adrenaline comedown. He stepped back.

Fiona touched her radio again. "Control, suspect Romanescu is in custody," she said. "Repeat, Nicolae Romanescu is under arrest. Shot once in the shoulder, conscious, disarmed. DS Barber transporting him to Leicester Royal Infirmary under armed guard. Over."

There was a crackle, and then the dispatcher's voice was replaced by Superintendent Henley's, unable to hide her relief. "Copy that, Fiona. Well done."

30

Carlos opened his office with Lady running in ahead of him. She seemed to have got over her trauma and was letting go of the separation anxiety that had plagued her since her ordeal.

Julie smiled up from her desk. “It’s good to see her looking like her normal self. And you’re a fast healer yourself.”

Carlos felt deep satisfaction that he and Fiona had finally put a criminal mastermind behind bars. The serious crimes unit’s reputation was riding high, particularly since Tony Hadden had returned from Spain and highlighted the work of a certain DI Cook in a two-page spread in the local paper.

Superintendent Henley had offered her a DCI step up, but Fiona loved being in the thick of things and would miss the day to day running of investigations, so she had asked for time to think about it.

Michael Kingsland had done a deal with the CPS to

ensure Nicolae Romanescu would be tried and convicted of his serious crimes, including a triple homicide.

Fiona had received an offer from her insurance company that would enable her to buy a neighbour's boat. She had resisted all suggestions of putting money down on a house, deciding she loved the boating community.

"Sorry you didn't get to catch Rachel's next stop in Montreal," Julie said.

"She understood and couldn't be happier about me catching Nicolae. There's always another port and in the meantime, I suppose you and I will just have to settle for each other, Lady," he replied, stroking her ears.

Lady barked as if understanding.

"Considering the trauma poor Lady went through, it's not a bad thing to have you around for longer," Julie said.

Carlos laughed. "She's milking the attention, if you ask me. And Sara's spoiling her rotten."

"I'm almost sorry she's working for Fiona and not you," Julie gave him a knowing look.

"You never know, we might get her yet."

Julie laughed as she returned her attention to the computer. "Not if DI Cook has anything to do with it."

"Speaking of Fiona. Are you happy for me to leave Lady here for a few hours? I promised Fiona I'd help her move onto her new boat."

"She's always welcome to stay with me, aren't you, Lady?"

Lady ran around and joined Julie at her desk, waiting for an inevitable treat that his PA kept in her drawer. Carlos shook his head; his dog could wrap all of them around her four paws, but she deserved lots of treats after her dreadful ordeal. Lady might have recovered from the trauma, but he hadn't. The only satisfaction was knowing that those responsible for their suffering were locked up. The charges against Nicolae should result in a full life sentence if there was any justice in the world.

EPILOGUE

No sooner had Carlos parked at the marina than a white van drove up and parked next to him.

Carlos recognised the vast frame behind the driver's wheel before he stepped out of the van.

"Hello Paul."

"Hi Carlos. Ready for this?"

"As ready as I'll ever be. This will be harder than solving crimes or giving sermons, you realise that don't you?"

Paul's shoulders heaved up and down as he guffawed. "I'm getting used to taking her orders."

Carlos raised an eyebrow, but Paul added nothing. He turned to unlock the back of the van. "Where is the boss lady?"

"Fiona's on board cleaning."

Carlos chuckled. "That'll be the first and last clean it gets. I suppose she wants to air it." The marijuana-smoking hippy couple who had inherited a boat had decided to sell up and travel after Fiona's was burned. Fiona also suspected they didn't wish to live so close to a detective inspector.

Paul grinned his good-natured grin as he heaved the first box out. Carlos followed suit, and they carried the boxes along the towpath to Fiona's new – or not so new – home. He'd been right in his guess; all the windows on the boat were open despite an early November frost.

"Anybody home?" Paul called.

Seconds later, Fiona emerged through the double doors, a happy gleam in her eyes. "I've just put the kettle on if you want a cuppa before you start."

"Better not. I've left the van doors open," said Paul. "Maybe when we've earned it." The knowing glances Fiona and Paul shared and the good-natured way they bantered over the next hour gave Carlos hope that his good friend might find love.

It wasn't long before other boat owners were helping, forming a chain as they passed boxes along from the car park to Fiona's new home. Perhaps the boating community was the right choice after all, Carlos thought. The expression 'many hands make light work' became a reality, and soon the boxes were on the boat or lined up on the towpath, ready to be moved and unpacked.

Once they were sitting on two long benches with hot drinks on the table, the trio relaxed.

"I wanted to tell you that Princess has moved to Bath and has settled into a nice mid-terraced house. She doesn't want me to share the address, but she asked me to thank you both," Paul said.

"We didn't really do anything; it was her Mr Cross who kept her safe," Fiona replied with a laugh.

"What happened to Ruby?" Carlos asked.

"She's scarpered back to Romania," Fiona said. "I just hope she stays on the right side of the law over there. Nicolae is still boasting he'll be free in no time, but it's all bluster."

"When's the trial?" Carlos asked.

"Early next year. We're going to need to ensure there's no jury tampering when it starts, but that's down to the CPS to sort. The prosecutor on the case is highly respected, so no issues there." She added. "Kingsland will still be charged, although the judge will consider his help in the matter of Nicolae. And Tyson Jerome admitted to his part in the riots and to assaulting a police officer, but denies any involvement in the murders, it was the guys working for Kingsland who did the killings under orders from Nicolae."

"That strengthens the case against him," Carlos said, feeling satisfied. "What about Hodge?"

"He's been charged with perverting the course of justice and malfeasance in a public office. The CPS are also considering whether there's enough evidence against him to charge him as an accessory relating to Sara's kidnap."

"I'm just happy those women's families will get the justice they deserve."

"And on that note," Paul said, "we've received an anonymous donation to be split between the three families."

Fiona's eyes widened. "Who from?"

"Did I mention the word anonymous, Fiona?" Paul laughed.

She gave his arm a playful thump. "I wonder if it was the

same person who donated all of this," she said, pointing to the boxes.

"I don't reveal sources, not even to the police," Paul replied.

Fiona looked at Carlos. "I've got a new case if you're interested?"

Carlos grinned. It was good to see Fiona looking so happy. He would save asking how they would go about tracing the mole, or moles, who tipped off Nicolae for another day. His phone pinged with a message from Rachel.

'Wish Fiona well from me and tell her no more investigations until I've seen my husband!'

He showed Fiona the phone. "Looks like you got your answer to the case question, if you were serious."

Fiona unsealed a box. "We'll see," she chuckled mischievously.

Paul shook his head, eyeing Fiona affectionately. "Do you never switch off, DI Cook?"

"Only when I'm asleep," she said. Carlos recognised the flinty determination flicker in her eyes for a moment and knew that she was as concerned about the residual corruption within the team as he was.

But this was a happy moment, and her face broke into a wide grin. "Now, how about helping me with unboxing?"

THE END

If you enjoyed this book and haven't read others in the

Carlos Jacobi series yet, start with the award winning novel: ***Body in the Woods***.

Check out what happened to Rachel after the disappointing phone call at the beginning of this book. ***Cruise Fountain Finale*** sees Rachel team up with a New York detective to investigate a passenger's murder.

Get five exclusive **FREE character dossiers** when you sign up for my crime fiction newsletter.

AFTERWORD

Thank you for reading *The Clock Tower Murders* the fourth book in the Carlos Jacobi PI series.

If you have enjoyed it, please leave an honest review on Amazon and/or any other platform you may use. I love receiving feedback from readers.

Get five exclusive **FREE character dossiers** when you sign up for my crime fiction newsletter.

ALSO BY DAWN BROOKES

CARLOS JACOBI PI

Body in the Woods #1

The Bradgate Park Murders #2

The Museum Murders #3

The Clock Tower Murders #4

RACHEL PRINCE MYSTERIES

A Cruise to Murder #1

Deadly Cruise #2

Killer Cruise #3

Dying to Cruise #4

A Christmas Cruise Murder #5

Murderous Cruise Habit #6

Honeymoon Cruise Murder #7

A Murder Mystery Cruise #8

Hazardous Cruise #9

Captain's Dinner Cruise Murder #10

Corporate Cruise Murder #11

Treacherous Cruise Flirtation #12

Toxic Cruise Cocktail #13

Cruise into Darkness #14

Cruise Fountain Finale #15

LADY MARJORIE SNELLTHORPE MYSTERIES

Death of a Blogger (Prequel Novella)

Murder at the Opera House #1

Murder in the Highlands #2

Murder at the Christmas Market #3

Murder at a Wimbledon Mansion #4

Murder in a Care Home #5

Murder at the Regatta #6

Murder on a Bus Tour #7

Book 8 coming soon 2026

MEMOIRS

Hurry up Nurse: memoirs of nurse training in the 1970s

Hurry up Nurse 2: London calling

Hurry up Nurse 3: More adventures in the life of a student nurse

ACKNOWLEDGMENTS

Thanks to my beta readers for their comments and suggestions, and for the time they dedicated to reading the early drafts, as well as to my ARC team – I couldn't do without you. A big thank you also goes to my editorial team.

I'm also immensely grateful to my immediate circle of family and friends, who remain patient when I'm absorbed in my fictional worlds. Thank you for your continued support in all my endeavours.

ABOUT THE AUTHOR

Award-winning author Dawn Brookes holds an MA in Creative Writing with Distinction and is the author of the Rachel Prince Mystery series, combining a unique blend of murder, cruising and medicine with a touch of romance. She has also written the Lady Marjorie Snellthorpe spinoff series and the Carlos Jacobi PI series.

Dawn has a 39-year nursing pedigree and takes regular cruise holidays, which she claims are for research purposes! She combines these passions with her Christian background and a love of clean crime in her writing.

Dawn's memoirs outlining her nurse training are available to buy: *Hurry up Nurse: memoirs of nurse training in the 1970s*, *Hurry up Nurse 2: London calling*, and *Hurry up Nurse 3: More adventures in the life of a student nurse.*

During her nursing career, Dawn worked as a hospital nurse, midwife, district nurse, and a community matron. Before turning to writing for a living, she had multiple articles published in professional journals and co-edited a nursing textbook.

Having grown up in Leicester she later moved to London and Berkshire, and now lives in Derby. Dawn has a passion for nature and loves animals, especially dogs. Animals will continue to feature in her children's books, as she believes caring for animals and nature helps children become kinder human beings.

"When not writing, I love curling up with a good book, walking, travelling and playing golf."

Printed in Dunstable, United Kingdom

77988411R00160